BOOK ONE: THE TRAPPER AND THE MISSING SPY

HERMAN P. HUNTER

www.hphunterwriter.com

CREDITS

Cover Design
Jason Robinson

Interior Formatting
www.helpingauthorseveryday.com

Beta Readers
The Wonderful Mrs. Herman Hunter, Richard Wilson, and Thomas Hyland

Editors
Krista Wagner and Matthew Bowman

Map Illustration
Gary Shipman

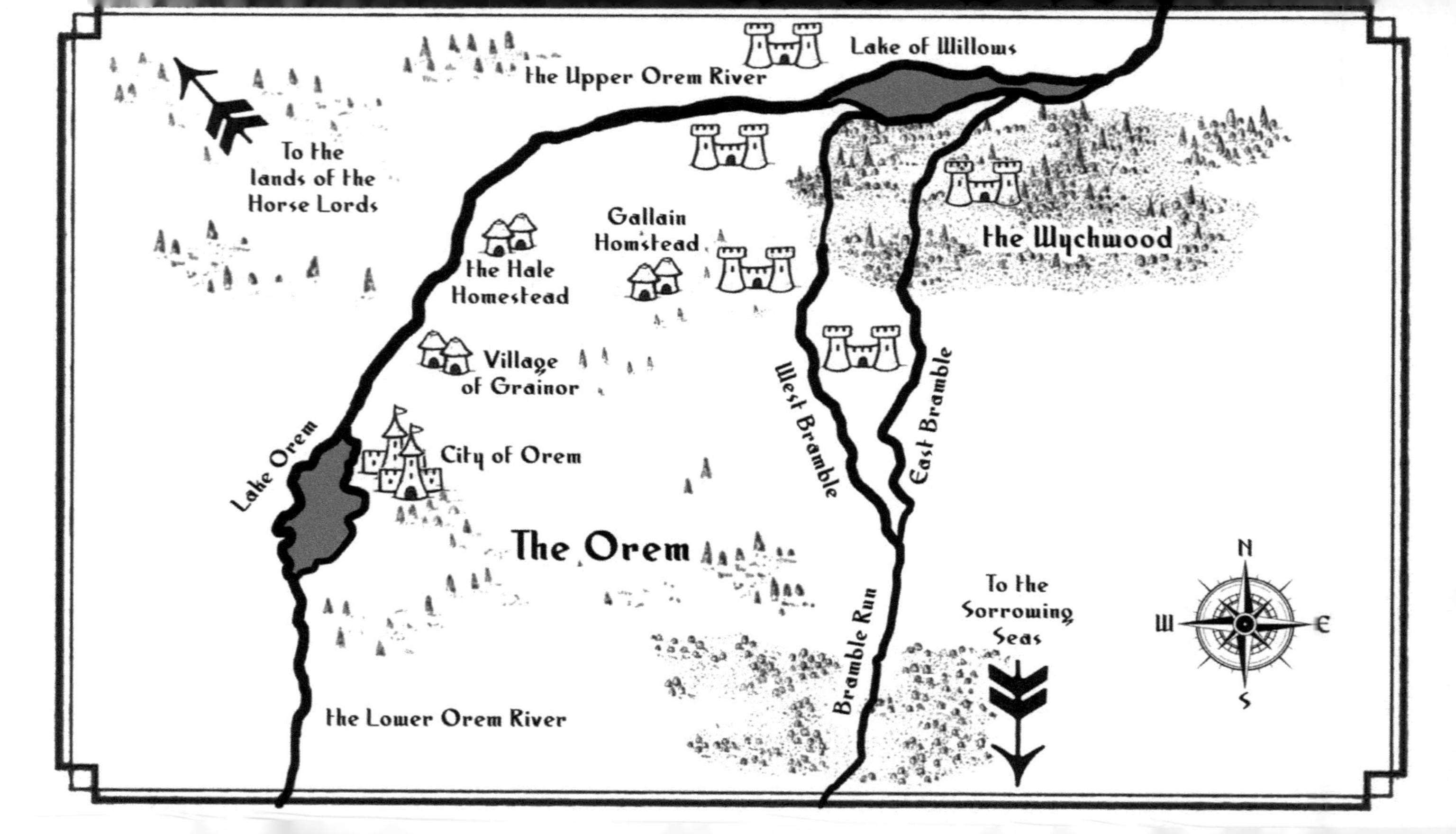
Lake of Willows
the Upper Orem River
To the
lands of the
Horse Lords
Gallain
Homstead
the Wychwood
the Hale
Homestead
Village
of Grainor
West Bramble
East Bramble
Lake Orem
City of Orem
The Orem
N
W
E
S
To the
Sorrowing
Seas
Bramble Run
the Lower Orem River

DEDICATION

THIS BOOK IS DEDICATED TO MY WIFE, MY LOVER, the mother of my children, and my partner in this life.

You stuck with me through cancer and the turbulent waters of my career.

When I was about to walk away from writing for a second and final time, you pulled me back and told me my talent was worth the risk.

You are my biggest fan and only true friend through the long years.

God has truly blessed me with your presence. And, as always, I love you.

FOREWORD

THIS IS THE STORY I NEVER INTENDED TO WRITE. Not that I didn't want to write it, though there were times I was wondering whether I should just scrap it and start over. It's just that I had a plan on how things were going to play out after I published *The Revenant and the Tomb*. A plan that didn't include this story.

What was the plan? Initially, it was to offer up *The Revenant and the Tomb* as a giveaway. This was inspired by a marketing ploy that any number of book marketing experts recommended. Then, I'd publish *The Wizard's Stone*. After that, a short series about a character named Merrith before the publication of a series I started writing well over two decades ago.

Well, that plan failed. Miserably.

I learned the hard way that if you are an unknown author, no one—and I do mean *no one*—wants anything you have to offer, even if you're giving it away. So, I published the novella.

That worked far better than any of the marketing advice that was offered on social media.

Despite this little hiccup, I continued to proceed with "the plan," and set about finishing *The Wizard's Stone*. During that period, I started receiving feedback on social media from readers who picked up my debut. I'm fielding questions like, "Is the next book the follow-up to The Revenant and the Tomb? Will Drahm be in the next book? I'd love to read more about Herodiani and Tulvgir!"

Given that I had no intention of writing another book with Halsedric, Herodiani, or Tolvgir as characters, it made my responses to these inquiries somewhat feeble and awkward. What was clear, however, was I had garnered a small following. And they wanted more. More of Halsedric.

Goodbye plan.

The Halsedric character was actually a prototype. I had an idea for a series of novellas that included a Halsedric-like character as part of an adventuring duo. *The Revenant and the Tomb* was only there to lay down a foundational framework for this character and as sort of a backstory for Asteroth. In short, Halsedric was disposable. And in the span of one book, he went from disposable to essential.

I'm a big believer in giving the fans what they want...to a point. Some will tell you that an author should prioritize following their vision before fan service. I disagree to a certain extent. If readers of my works want more, I should endeavor to give them more. I started to view the Halsedric character in a new light. He might not have been the character I wanted to move forward with, but I could use him to move *backward.* Even though I'm writing *to* a planned series, I could use Halsedric to explore some of the background lore of the world in which my stories are set. With that in mind, while I was gearing up for the release of *The Wizard's Stone*, I set about the task of writing this story.

It has taken over a year of wrangling and wrestling with this story to get it to this stage. I've had people read it and re-read it. I've scrapped sections and started over. My initial expectations were that the final story was to be a book roughly the size of *The Wizard's Stone.* When I was done filling in all the little details, I had a much grander work than I initially envisioned. When it went to the beta readers, it was over 100,000 words. Not huge when compared to many fantasy books out there, but a respectable size. The biggest complaint people had about *The Revenant and the Tomb* was that, by the time they were done, they wanted more. So...this is "more."

And then others started publicly praising me for my skill at writing shorter, less expansive books. No, I'm not joking.

The plan I once had? Well, it's been put through the shredder.

I still have an eye on publishing some of those projects I have in a sort of literary limbo. I also have other stories that I want to write, and I'd like to revive the Halsedric origin story. But I don't think I'll be holding fast to any plan from this point forward. Yes, I intend to write more books. Depending on how these next two books are received, I'll probably write more Halsedric stories. I already have three more held in stasis somewhere in my memory.

Now, you may have noticed I said "books" earlier. Given the size of the story I wrote, I decided to take a risk and divide *The Revenant and the Cult* into two distinct books. Whether it was a wise move or not, only time will tell. I will tell you that I agonized over this decision for months. My wife got tired of me constantly bringing up the subject. Several factors went into my decision some financial, others stylistic. In the end, it was the story itself that made the decision. The final manuscript read like two distinct stories, despite the fact that they were one cohesive tale. This unacknowledged fact nagged at me throughout the entire development and editing process. Splitting the book in two, however, left me with a rather abrupt ending in the first book, and an abrupt beginning for the next. In the end, I decided to go with my gut.

This story starts about a year after the end of *The Revenant and the Tomb*, making it a direct successor to the previous work. I'm hesitant to call these three books a "series," as I've always sort of envisioned Halsedric's place in my literary cosmos as being more episodic in nature. If I revive my first attempt at writing him—and this is a distinct possibility—his stories will not arrive sequentially. I rather favor that concept. It seems like everyone is doing their epic fantasy series, so why try and compete in that space? Why not do something a little...different?

So now you know probably more than you ever wanted to know about this book and its second installment. I wrote it for you, the fans, and included some of the things requested of me. Not because I felt compelled to do so, but because you wanted more. That's the whole point of all of this.

I sincerely hope you enjoy *The Revenant and the Cult*. Both parts of it.

P.S.—Pay attention to the prologue. It's setting the foundation for several stories to come. Including one you may have already read.

PROLOGUE

ATOP A ROCKY RISE, THE CRUMBLING REMAINS OF a once mighty fortress clawed at the night's sky. A canopy of clouds diffused the light of the full moon, contrasting with the jagged tips of black stone that stood against the pale aura of the moonlight. The moon provided just enough light to reveal the dark points of walls long thrown down and the shattered remains of high towers destroyed long ago when the fortress fell.

This was a place of dread and misery. A long-forgotten memory of an age of darkness and despair, where ghosts of the vile and tormented alike continued to haunt the stony carcass. One where the cries of the tortured could still be heard in the very stones, their misery saturating the earth. Yet even in its ruined state, it still stood defiant, like a broken and mangled fist that shook in rage against Creation's maker.

Below, standing in the woeful shadow of the ruins, shrouded forms gathered. On a level plateau, vague figures were arrayed in a line, all dressed in black, their identities further obscured by cloaks and hoods. Behind them opened a great yawning maw in the rock face of a sheer cliff, the entrance flanked on each side by fire, as if Perdition itself lay beyond. Flames, whose forked and twisting nature lifted skyward, hissed, spit, and roared their discontent. Around the raised plateau, the ruins of the lower fortress lay. Walls overturned, stones broken and cast down. Sparse rubble collected into piles, swept away to make level the ground on which fifty mysterious men gathered. An ominous scene amidst the darkness, decay, and unnerving silence.

In the distance, the shapes of trees rose, barely visible beneath the scattered rays of the dampened moon. They hid this ancient blight from the world beyond, the remote wilderness providing an adequate shelter for the sinister gathering.

Yet, the most unnerving aspect of all was the pervasive quiet. Those who gathered did not speak and the only sound that could be heard came from the pop and crackle of fire. There were no calls of night creatures, no faraway hoots from owls. The long, mournful wail of wolves often heard in the wilderness did not echo in the distance. All was silence and darkness, dead and oppressive.

In the distant dark, other forms approached from the west, moving toward the gathering along an ascending lane. At first, they were little more than vague outlines against the shadows. As the stray light of the fire caught them, their numbers were revealed, four in all. Four shapes ascended to the plateau in a slow and cautious march. Their heads moved this way and that, the travelers on alert and wary of what might linger in the shadows that surrounded the lane on which they trod. For something did dwell there among the lower ruins. Something that stalked them like prey, scrambling over piles of rubble and vanishing behind the cover. Dark forms, indistinct, veiled by the night, letting the terrain conceal them as they tracked these unknown and unbidden travelers.

The closer they came to the fire, the clearer the features of the wanderers became. Each was roughly the size of a man, though their features varied. Two of them were tall and lean. A cuirass of leather covered their torsos, their lower thighs protected by leathery straps that hung down like aprons. Articulated strips covered portions of their shoulders and arms, and leggings of leather protected their legs. Swords hung from their waists, secured by straps slung around their shoulders. Long thready hair as black as pitch hung down from their crowns, their prominent horns ascending from the fore of their brows. Long spikes that rose from flesh and bone, curved back at a slight angle, and twisting slightly along their axis. Sallow complected, they appeared sickly and pale as the firelight revealed their features. Narrow lids covered eyes whose color was like blood and fire, the flame behind them fueled by an unquenchable wrath instilled in them by their makers. These were Yerch, as remembered in ancient tales. The first of their kind, and—by many accounts—the most dangerous of their breed.

Two others followed behind. One was a brute of a creature, very much of the same make as the other two but with notable differences. It was broader and taller than its compatriots, its skin mottled both black and green. Wearing a shirt of ebon mail and greaves of black iron, its shoulders were adorned with pieces cast from thick iron that was studded with curved thorns along their face. It too bore a sword whose sheath was fashioned from the hide of a boar. The pommel of the weapon resembled the claw of a raptor, whose sharp digits clutched a stone of pure black.

The fourth and final Yerch was smaller by far than the other three. Pale like two of its vile brethren, it was slender and hairless. Its garb was a rude mix of hide and tanned leather with rough spun woolen breeches covering its calves and thighs. What horns erupted from its brow were less prominent than the other three, being thinner and shorter. Yet, the one feature that distinguished it from its companions was an orderly configuration of wicked-seeming runes, engraved into its hide with dark brown ink. Arranged in neat columns and rows, they covered the creature from head to foot, as if the whole of its body was dedicated to some occult spell whose meaning had been wisely lost. A conjuration whose trauma was mercifully forgotten by the world with the passing of darker days. About its neck hung a necklace of thin bones ending in a bleached skull of some small creature. Each vacant void in the skull was affixed with a red translucent stone as dark as newly spilled blood.

The Ageless had a name for these queer and diminutive Yerch, so named Ogogalath in the tongue of the Fair Folk. These were the most feared among their kind, being the embodiment of a greater turpitude. Dreaded and despised, it was a creature sought out and slain upon sight. For the Elanni knew all too well the terrors these fiends could conjure.

Of these four Yerch, there was one feature they all shared. Upon their brow, each bore a distinctive mark raised from their flesh as if it were scarring from a brand. A mark that was as simple as it was enigmatic—an arrangement of two rings, one intertwined with the other.

As the Yerch approached the enigmatic figures in black, they gazed at the assemblage with a restrained sort of puzzlement. While the identities of the figures in black were hidden by hoods and cloaks, that was not all they wore. Many among the throng wore masks, also black, covering their faces from nose to chin. The only part that hinted at their humanity was their eyes. Some of the face coverings were made of simple cloth tied at the back, while others were elaborately carved from wood and painted black, the graven images etched thereon being nightmarish in their imagery and expression. Aside from this one detail, the congregants were uniform in dress. With faces obscured, they were alike in appearance such that they could almost be copies of one another. Black. Plain. Anonymous. All save but three.

Of these three, one might find it difficult to call them men. Middling in height, they too were garbed in black, though their cloaks differed from those of the others. Something about them glinted in the orange-red glow of the fire, having the appearance of being made up of a multitude of individual feathers. This was also true of their long dark manes that fell from their crowns, for they too seemed to be mingled with ebony down. Yet, it was their countenance that truly defined them, for their skin was as pale as the moonlight itself. Serpentine eyes with sickly yellow irises stared at the onlookers with an intense, unblinking vigilance. Their noses pushed out like beaks, unnaturally long and hooked. And when they moved, it was quick and abrupt, like the movements of a bird.

The four Yerch slowed to a halt several paces from the line of dark-clad congregants. The burly Yerch stepped forward and gazed to the left and the right, inspecting the crowd gathered there, the moments dragging on for an uncomfortably long time.

Impatient with the inattentiveness of their hosts, the great dark Yerch sneered, its thin lips exposing a set of teeth that were yellowed, broken, and disorderly. "Is this how an emissary and ally is welcomed? Threats and silence?" Its hot red eyes made a quick sidelong stare at the line of forms that had gathered to greet them.

The creature's answer was more silence.

From the center of the line, one of the cloaked men stepped forward, wordless, a bare hand extended, the fingers of it silently bidding them to draw closer. The four Yerch gazed at one another in bewilderment, each seemingly confused as to whether they should do as they were bid. Then, with furtive steps, the Yerch moved forward in unison. As they neared the center of the line of men, it slowly broke, some circling around the grim visitors, causing each of the horned fiends to twist about with anger and alarm.

Standing alone, the hooded figure raised his hands once more to bid the Yerch to halt. There, where they stood, more details could be seen at the opening in the face of the cliff. The entrance was engraved about the fringes; faux beams carved and shaped from the natural stone of the cliff face. These rose upward and inward at a slight angle, connecting to a third vertical bar also shaped from the stone of the cliff. Within each hewn beam, horrid runes were etched, the stony depressions barely visible in the available light. Contained by these decorative beams was a great, black yawning void, hinting at a much larger space within the cliff face.

The man who commanded the Yerch in silence was taller than the rest of the assembly. The fabric of his garb had a finer make than those of the others, his robes seeming to shimmer in the light of the fire. Stuffed in a sash cinched about his waist was a weapon of sorts—a dagger whose hilt stuck up from a crude sheath made of hide. Standing only a few paces away from the four Yerch, his hands pulled back the hood that hid his face. Open sleeves slid down along his forearms, exposing pale skin that had not seen sunlight for some time; no mask adorned his face. Dark eyes stared out arrogantly from beneath his brows, his face long and his head shaved. On his lips was the hint of a sinister grin, as if he knew a dread secret unknown to all who gathered there.

Metal ground against stone as the large, mottled Yerch knelt on the ground. It turned its head to the Ogogalath and growled, "Summon forth the master."

The other two Yerch laid hands on both the horns and shoulders of their leader, maintaining a firm grip. The Ogogalath approached from behind. From a pouch tied to its belt, the Ogogalath withdrew a single stone that was pure black in the glow of the firelight. Its sinewy fingers wrapped around the object, palming the stone tightly in its fist. With its free hand, it pressed its fingers and palm onto the crown of the dark Yerch.

Eyes closed, head back, the shaman began to chant, mostly whispers at first. Over and over the Ogogalath repeated the strain, each round increasing in intensity. The hard and guttural tongue of the creature growled and grumbled as if it were spewing an endless font of blasphemies in a tongue too foul to repeat.

The kneeling Yerch began to struggle. The more the shaman chanted, the greater the intensity and the thrashing of the companion on whom its hand lay. The others who held down their leader struggled to maintain their grip. Before long, the words of the Ogogalath were like vile shouts into the air, the Yerch leader letting loose a long, baying scream. A pitiful sound suggestive of beasts just before the slaughter. As the ritual continued, the world around them was drowned out by chanting and screams reminiscent of some ancient thing rising from abysmal depths. The diffuse moonlit aura in the overcast seemed to dim in reply.

Then came a profound silence.

The struggling ceased. For an instant, all existence seemed to hold its breath. The two Yerch who restrained their comrade pulled away, reacting out of fear. Yet, the Ogogalath maintained its grip on the scalp of the large Yerch, steam leaking out from the tight digits of the hand that clutched the stone. Eyes still clenched shut, the Ogogalath inhaled as if drawing its first breath.

Then, the kneeling Yerch opened its eyes. The red irises and the sickly yellow that surrounded them were now painted a glossy black. Whatever life those terrible orbs once held were now supplanted by something else. Something beyond mere flesh and bone. A dark, menacing aura projected from them, revealing a horrific majesty that did not exist before.

The head of the Yerch leader turned to one side then the other, its hands balled into fists. All the while, the Ogogalath's fingers seemed fused to the back of the leader's head. Eventually, those cold black eyes fixed on the priest. And when the large Yerch spoke, it did so in unison with the Ogogalath, as if one dominant voice spoke from both.

"I am here," said the Yerchish pair. The two harsh voices of the conjoined Yerch mingled with a third that transcended both. It was a voice as deep as the ocean depths, and as dark as the secret desires of lustful men.

“Summon him, priest,” commanded the possessed Yerch, lifting its finger and pointing to the bald man who stood patiently before him.

The priest nodded. Casting off his cloak, he pulled the dagger from his belt. The blade of the knife was faceted, rough, and shone like black glass. Holding up the crude weapon to his face, he eyed the edge, scanning each crag where the excess stone was napped away. Despite its primitive construction, the blade itself was thinner and sharper than any such implement of steel. Heaving deep, eyes wide, the hand of the priest trembled. Once haughty eyes now seemed tinged with fear as his fingers flexed around the wooden handle of the stone knife. For a time, he paused, perhaps as if mustering the courage for the task he was assigned. Slowly he turned to the open maw in the face of the rock behind him before breathing deep one last time. Afterward, he made a slow path to the gloom that lay beyond the opening, disappearing into the darkness.

Sounds were heard coming from that void in the stone. Horrible rending sounds followed by the sickening noise of gurgling. A faint cry was noted, born of pain, before a dread silence fell. A quiet so deep and terrible that it felt as if the world itself were ending.

From the impenetrable darkness there came a figure in the vague shape of a man, whose eyes shone with a pale, menacing light. As it stepped out from the cave, the details were made clearer.

It was the priest who entered there only moments before. Yet now, a great jagged gash rent the skin of his throat, curving from ear to ear. His pallid skin was now like bleached bone. The distinct mist of a shadow formed about him, the ribbons of it wrapping around the wicked gash, a crown of black fume hovering over the man's shorn head. Soon, all of the congregants in attendance fell to their knees as if in terrified obedience. Some fell to their faces, fearful to lift their eyes. Even the two Yerch who flanked their companions looked down or away from the terrible reverence that emanated from the broken priest, this oozing, nameless evil whose likes rarely came forth from the deep shadows. When it spoke, it was like a shout, a whisper, and a scream conjoined.

"Why hast thou summoned me?" said the transformed priest, his slow and purposeful walk coming to an end mere paces away from the gathered Yerch. "Why doest thou linger in the West when thy throne lies in the East? Why doest thou disturb me in my shelter?"

"Here I have come, that you might remember your vow. To aid me in the task I must do," uttered the joined Yerch.

"To what end?" Head back, the figure of the priest gazed down in seeming condescension at the Yerch.

"To what end?" The mouth of the dark Yerch curled up in a snarl and its face churned with a distant rage as the being that possessed the conjoined creatures spat out the question. “It is now my time and a vow you have taken. As you have aided Hashocar, so you shall aid me.”

“Thou shalt fail,” replied the priest, his face calm and expressionless.

“Shall I?”

“It has been foreseen.”

“Has it?” The expression of the Yerch changed, turning coy if not slightly amused. As if the thing that possessed it knew something the other didn’t. When the possessed priest did not reply, that coy expression turned to one of rage. With an accusatory finger, it spat curses through quivering lips and teeth like a viper might spit venom. “Oathbreaker! Snake! A covenant we all made long ago, and now you turn your back on your brethren!”

“Curse me if thou wilt,” answered the priest. “It will change naught the fate laid upon us all. Thy time is at hand, my time is yet to come. Our bond shall not undo our fates, nor shall I imperil such plans I have set to motion. Seek ye the others if aid thou needst.”

“There are no others,” snarled the Yerch.

“There is one,” answered the priest.

“Mindless and heedless he is,” replied the Yerch. “This you know.”

The mists about the neck of the priest coiled and curled as the pale glowing dots for eyes stared patiently at the Yerch. As if whatever presence possessed the dead man was deep in contemplation. Then it spoke once more.

"Show me that which thou hast revealed. Only then shall I grant thee aid."

"In what form shall your aid be delivered?"

A tense silence followed as the two figures glared at one another, as if their stares grappled with that of the other. Both were resolute and unafraid, neither willing to yield.

"Show me what thou offerest and aid I will deliver to thee."

The dark Yerch growled. "Were it not for me, you would not have that tame dog who comes to heel when you call. Or have you forgotten?"

"I will not lay my plans at thy altar, only to fall into ruin when thou fallest. A bond I must fulfill, and so I shall. Yet, I will not do so blindly. Show me. Only then shall I grant thee aid."

The eyes of the Yerch narrowed, and its lips drew close, almost into a scowl. For a time, whatever power possessed the creature considered the bargain.

The Yerch spoke this time, resigned, but with anger and iron lacing each of its words. "I will deliver that which you bid. And when I have done so, you will hand over those that follow you, and they shall do my bidding. Lest you be cursed and undone. So, it is agreed?"

Then with a sly smirk on its lips, the Yerch spoke spiteful and haughty. "Oh, great Maelzozael."

The eyes of the priest opened wide as if a grave and profane thing had just been spoken. He recoiled then raised one arm in the air, fingers outstretched. From the palm grew a spike of shadow and pale malevolent light. Hazy at first, it took the vague form of a sword, the fingers of the priest closing about the hilt. Then, as swift as lightning strikes the earth, the sword fell, cleanly severing the head of the kneeling Yerch from its body.

At once, the Yerch conjurer fell back dazed, the head of its dead comrade still fused to its fingers. As the headless body of the Yerch leader fell forward, vines, twisted and terrible, broke from the ground. They bound the feet of the remaining Yerch and wound around their calves. Woody tendrils and creepers rose and rapidly entangled the remaining horned fiends, binding their hands, and wrapping around their shoulders. Eventually, the pale pink and brown extensions penetrated their mouths, stifling their cries and holding them fast.

Powerless, struggling to break free, the three Yerch worked fruitlessly to escape their bonds. As they did, Maelzozael stepped forward and drew near to one of the tall, lean creatures.

The sword the priest held vanished like dust in a maelstrom. The insidious glow from his eyes scanned one of his helpless victims with an inquisitive, almost scholarly expression.

"Ah, thou art an ancient thing," said Maelzozael, scanning one of the pale Yerch up and down. “Wrought by the will of Hashocar.” Lifting his pale fingers, it traced the mark it bore on its forehead, seeming to relish the act.

“What grim glories thou hast seen? What depravations hast thou suffered in our fall? Exquisite and sorrowful,” he said as his cold fingers caressed the pale-yellow skin of the bound creature, running along the length of its jaw.

The Yerch tried to pull away, its eyes bulging in terror. The knot that penetrated its mouth stifled both words and screams.

“Yet, thou art his creature now,” muttered Maelzozael. With a sigh of disappointment, he added, “And I pity thee that thine days, so long suffered, end here.”

CHAPTER ONE

"FOLK DON'T TAKE KINDLY TO STRANGERS IN these parts, young sir."

The words of the alewife repeated themselves in Halsedric's mind as he sat there on the bench. Keeping a strict watch on the door of the trader's hovel just across the lane, he was waiting for a man to appear. A man of middling height and narrow eyes. A figure dressed in wool and leather with short dark hair that was crudely cut.

It was the owner of the alehouse that issued the warning, even as she plucked the coins he had laid out on the table. Two silver discs upon which was embossed the face of some noble or king, flanked by sheaves of wheat. He knew the name of the coin, but not what the image represented. Those tiny details tended to change over the long years as generations came and went, borders shifted, and dynasties rose and fell.

Halsedric was already on his fourth cup of ale, a question burning in his mind, demanding an answer. “Woman?” Halsedric called out to the alewife. “Why then does an inn reside next to your establishment if strangers are not welcome?” His eyes never once left that door to the hovel, even as he took a sip of his ale from the earthenware mug.

“What say you, young man?” answered the mistress of the establishment in her warbling voice. The sound of a woman of advanced age, still spry even as her body was being slowly eroded by time. Diminutive by any standard of measure, a plain earthen dress made of rough cloth wound around her fragile frame bound at the waist with a leather sash. Her ashen gray hair was pulled back and bound into a tight bun behind her head, exposing the whole of her weathered and wrinkled face.

She might have been beautiful in her youth. Or not. It was hard to tell in her waning years. The travails of life had not only weathered her skin, but left gaps in her smile where some of her teeth were lost. Despite her stubborn defiance in the face of aging, her battle against time did not come without a cost. She stood slightly bent, her feet scuffing the dirt with a distinctive shuffling gait. Withered and age-spotted arms cradled the earthen pitcher, half-filled with ale. Her hands trembled slightly as they moved, the deftness of her fingers much diminished in these, her final days.

Setting his cup down on the weathered table, he took a moment to twist back and around behind him. Extending a finger to point to a wall, he answered her. "The inn. What purpose has an inn when strangers are not welcome here?" Despite his curiosity, he did not wait for an answer. He returned to his watch.

"Merchants and such," she answered. Halsedric could hear her feet shuffle against the dirt as she took two small steps forward. "Some be known to folk hereabouts."

The ale house where Halsedric lingered was one of those buildings whose foundations were built of stone and mortar, much like the inn next to it. Unlike the inn, it was an open-air establishment, a skeletal frame of timbers that held up a pitched roof, set into a low wall. The shade from the hot sun and the spring breeze made the alehouse a pleasant place to enjoy his drink, though he wondered secretly what was done to keep out the elements during the deeps of winter. Nonetheless, with no walls to block his view, it made it a simple task for him to keep an eye on the rest of the village.

The absence of walls had drawbacks of its own. If he could look out, others could look in. He could almost feel the gaze of some of the villagers on him, the stranger in their midst. It even crossed his mind that the attentive nature of the alewife was more than just a desire to attend her one and only customer.

Others were also out and about at this noontime hour, though the village, in general, was sleepy and quiet. Halsedric caught a glance of a woman filling an earthenware jug at the central well, a child in tow. He could hear the rhythmic ring of a smith's hammer not far away, the braying of an ass, and the murmurings of various folk as they went about their business. Each of them, he assumed, shot a quick and suspicious glance at the youthful man with tight blonde locks drinking alone in the local ale house.

The ale he drained from his cup was crude but satisfying, despite the odor being sour and bready. The old woman crafted her brew in a weathered shed, not too far from where he sat. The brown liquid fermented in stony vats, the frothing scum floating on top typically skimmed off during the process. Such practices and establishments were common in the region. The ale he consumed was a far cry from the refined wines of the Elanni he had sipped only a few months before. Silver chalices filled to the brim with a dark burgundy liquid brought for his refreshment as he delved the libraries of the Ageless. Seeking to learn more about the enigmatic evil that called itself *Asteroth*.

While the ale was an uncouth beverage, by comparison, it had its own appeal. It was an honest drink made with what was plentiful in the region. A hearty and fortifying draught served to those who toiled and sweat beneath a pitiless sun. And in that regard, it was the equal of any vintage known.

This was not his first visit to the region of the Orem, though it had been some time. West of the Aranach and north of the Sorrowing Sea, it was the furthest end of a region the Elanni so named the Aufelinur, and men called The Marmaedwe. A long expanse of steppes, grasslands, and marsh-laden moors, punctuated by anomalous formations of upthrust and fractured stone mounds and clusters of trees. A region of farms and herds, plowmen and shepherds, and scattered villages like the one he now occupied, where dirt, grass, dung, and stone were far more plentiful than lumber as evidenced by the various dwellings that formed the village proper.

Taking another moment, he scanned the village again, having the vague and itchy feeling he was being watched. His eyes traced the course of the single dirt track that was the main road of the settlement, investigating the disordered and varied buildings and dwellings that lined the crude avenue. Like so many settlements in this region, it was a place poor in timber. What wood could be had was not of the quality one might want for framing and trussing. The people who occupied this region were reliant on things like rock, mortar, thatch, and sod. The inn was one of the few buildings where wood was predominant, though its foundation was that of fieldstone and mortar. Much of the exterior was covered in wattle and daub, in need of a fresh coat of lime wash. The rest of the dwellings here were those whose walls were made of compressed clay and dirt, hard-packed and dried, or large blocks of sod, stacked atop one another and congealed into a dense uniform mass by a good rain. Thatched roofs with extended eaves protected the walls from the abundant rains, as well as providing welcome shade from the sun overhead. Some of the other dwellings had tiles of fired earth and clay covering their roof, decorative and orderly with low-sloping angles. In and among these various structures, the villagers went about their daily lives, more than a few casting a suspicious eye or two at the stranger with pale eyes and golden hair. A stranger whose vigil across from the trader's hovel did not go wholly unnoticed. Some, it seemed, took a keener interest in Halsedric's presence than others.

Of these interested parties, Halsedric took note, his gaze lingering long. Like many who lived here, they wore hats that were wide-brimmed and woven from straw. When they noticed his stare, they moved on.

"More, if you please." Halsedric placed his empty cup next to him on the table, making it easier for the alewife to refill. She shuffled along the ground, groaning due to the weight of the pitcher as she refilled his cup.

The man Halsedric waited for—the one with the narrow eyes and dark hair—was a woodsman and trapper of game, known to frequent the outlying villages of the city of Orem. An individual who was often sought after by many of the farmers in the outlying homesteads. On farms, chickens were always under threat from foxes and the more aggressive rodents of the moors, and masses of deer were the scourge of any farmer who grew grains. He was a man who thinned the herds of rampaging deer and blunted the onslaught of the pernicious wolves that roamed and hunted the outlying hills.

Were it not for his important task, Halsedric might have relished the beauty of the village and the landscape that surrounded it. For nearly the passing of a moon, he and Herodiani had set a watch on the village, waiting for this particular man to arrive. A man now hiding in the hovel of a trader while Halsedric sipped his sour ale. What little he saw of the joyous spring bloom was tempered by the grave seriousness of his mission. He was not one for sitting idly or waiting for events to unfold.

"More ale?" asked the alewife.

Lost in his own world, Halsedric continued his vigil, taking another sip after a time.

"I've half a mind to ask you to leave," protested the proprietress. "We've seen enough troubles in these parts as of late. And you've got the feel of a man that trouble follows."

Halsedric paused, then set down his cup. To any other patron, such remarks might have caused offense. Not to him. They were insightful in their own way. For, indeed, he was a man whose path cut treacherous waters, trouble following in the wake. His eyes drifted away from the door and stared into the dark contents of that glazed earthenware cup. Then, he scanned the village once more, noting more than a few people taking an interest in him. At once, he drained what remained in his mug before setting it down on the splintered, porous grain of the tabletop. With one more swift glance at the trading house door, he turned slightly on his bench and addressed the old woman.

"By what name are you called?"

The alewife shuffled back a pace, those thin, fragile arms clutching tighter the pitcher of ale, as if doing so could stave off some sort of imminent attack. With wide and fearful eyes, she answered, "Folks `bout here call me Mother Jade."

Pulling a leather pouch from his belt, he went about untying the leather strings that bound it closed. Palming it in one hand, his fingers pushed into the lip and pried it open. Inside was revealed a small cache of silver and gold coins, each of them stamped with the mark of the realm. From them, he collected four silver pieces and set them on the table in a small pile.

Mother Jade's expression changed from fear to a sort of greedy curiosity as her eyes fixed upon those coins. "Aye?"

Halsedric's head bowed as he lashed the leather ties about the lip of the purse. "I have a small task for you. If you are willing."

There was silence from Mother Jade, signaling hesitancy. Halsedric twisted further around, the corner of his eye catching the blurry form of the woman in the periphery of his vision.

"Aye?" she said again, her voice cracking slightly as she answered him.

"There is a man in the establishment over there." His head turned quickly back and nodded in the direction of the trader's establishment. "A man with dark hair, trading skins for gold and goods."

"Roe's his name," answered Mother Jade, her voice soft and slightly indecisive.

Halsedric continued to speak. "I need you to relay a message."

"And what would that be?" The proprietress clutched her pitcher even tighter in her withered arms.

"You know where the stand of willows grows? On the crest of the hilltop just outside the village?" Halsedric motioned ahead of him the pouch of coins pinched between his fingers.

"Aye," said Mother Jade with a nod. Her voice, however, took on a suspicious and defiant tone. "Folks know Roe 'round here. If'n there be trouble—"

"No trouble," interrupted Halsedric, his voice calm and reasoned. He paused for a moment, eyeing Mother Jade before continuing. "Tell him a friend of Wolland waits for him. Tell him to meet me at the crest of that hill, when he has concluded his business."

"I ain't lookin' for no trouble! I'm too old to be—"

The old woman's rebuke was halted when Halsedric opened his purse once more. From it, he took three more silver coins and two made of gold. These, he set down with the others, the sound of them making a dull clink against the rough and splintered timbers of the tabletop. In the silence that followed, he set about retying the string of the purse, eventually tucking the whole of it back into his belt. Reaching behind him, he grabbed his cloak as he shifted on his seat. Straddling the bench now, he set the lump of his well-worn cloak in his lap before looking up at the dumbfounded expression painted on the face of Mother Jade.

The eyes of the old woman went wide as she stared at the small pile of coins, her thin eyebrows arched like the peaks of a cathedral. As he rose from his seat, Halsedric offered a slight smile.

Throwing his cloak over his shoulder as he lifted his leg from around the other side of the bench, he spoke. "No trouble, woman. I assure you. Tell him."

Halsedric clumsily walked around the proprietress as she continued to ogle at the coins left on the table. Passing her on his way to the exit, Halsedric halted, and he gently laid a hand on her shoulder. Through the rough cloth of her simple gown, he could feel the fragile and diminutive frame of the crone, thin aging flesh over brittle bones.

He removed his hand before he passed, his boots thumping the plain dirt floor as he departed the establishment.

Stepping out into the clear sunlit day, he looked both ways before heading westward, fully understanding that now he was the sole focus of the village. As he casually strolled to the edge of the village, he could feel the wary eyes on the back of his neck. If he had hoped to come and go with scant notice, he had failed miserably.

Yet, his visit was not entirely fruitless. Things were as the reports and dispatches said. Mother Jade's behavior confirmed those suspicions. Something was amiss in these parts.

CHAPTER TWO

BENEATH THE WEEPING BOUGHS OF A WILLOW ON the hilltop, not far on the outskirts of the village, Halsedric waited in eager anticipation for a meeting. The drooping boughs of the tree made for good cover and a welcome shade from the bright sun overhead. The tendrils and their leaves swayed in a lazy dance when the breezes blew. There was something about the movement of the wind through the boughs of the willows that brought a sense of peace to him. Whether it was the swaying of the limbs or the sighing of the leaves, he wasn't altogether sure. They brought back memories of a life now long lost. Of summers fishing with his uncle or whiling away the hours daydreaming as opposed to tending to his studies. The long, thin leaves of willows were a staple of summer and shade for a restless youth.

Many such trees grew here, left mostly untouched by the people who inhabited these lands. The harder, more beneficial trees had been felled long ago, most of them used in the various constructions that made the village. Willow was a poor material for structural elements. The locals relied on it as a fuel, but only out of need. Many used a type of cake known as Herdcoal—a mixture of dried dung and coal dust—for their everyday uses. Those residents of means merely purchased actual coal, mined and imported from the northern highlands and mountains. It explained the ashen taste of the bread Halsedric consumed when he visited, and the dark smoke that curled from the chimneys and ovens when the dawn broke over the horizon.

The willows still had their uses, as these small rural communities used whatever could be found for their needs. The bark was used in concoctions to reduce fever and pain. The wood pulp was woven into nets, often sold in the city of Orem. The branches of these trees fell easily in the summer storms and cluttered the ground. Oft times these shattered limbs were collected and fabricated into wood handles for tools, or transformed into shaved strips that were woven into baskets.

For Halsedric, they acted as a screen of sorts, allowing him to monitor the comings and goings of the village in relative obscurity. Yet, there was one figure that garnered his attention the most. A solitary figure on a single mount, causing Halsedric's brow to furrow momentarily. The man he sought was a trapper—an itinerant figure who lived on or near the homesteads he serviced. Such a man would have two horses, the second being the beast which bore the burden of the goods he traded from time to time. It did not take Halsedric long to deduce the reason for this discrepancy. Either the man was cautious, fearing he might be waylaid in such an encounter, or he was not the man Halsedric was seeking. This latter thought troubled Halsedric the most.

As horse and rider ascended the slope of the hill, Halsedric stepped out from the thin, drooping branches and the slender elongated leaves to stand in the open. Despite the rising heat of the day, he continued to wear his cloak. The garment hid the sword that he carried, his left hand resting on the hilt beneath the cloth. A solitary figure waiting on that hill, he knew that his presence could be interpreted as being ominous and threatening under the wrong circumstances. While it wasn't his wish to appear in such a manner, it wasn't something that was altogether undesired.

The rider halted for a moment and looked up the hill, noticing at once Halsedric's presence. When he resumed his progress, his direction changed, turning to Halsedric's left, giving him a wide berth before cresting the top. By now, Halsedric could glean scant details of the rider and his effects. He was a younger man, perhaps in his thirties. The breeches he wore were that of leather, most likely doeskin, bound tight at his waist with a cord. A matching vest, also of a ruder construction, covered his chest and abdomen, with a stained and dirty shirt of linen beneath. His sleeves were rolled up to expose his sinewy forearms, one way to escape the heat of the day. Set atop a chestnut mare, his saddle was fashioned from wood with horns protruding from the front and rear. Padded cloth, layered and quilted covered the seat both atop and below, secured to the animal by woven cloth straps. While one hand clutched the reins, the other was kept at his side, hidden from Halsedric's view. It wasn't difficult to determine that a weapon was readied in the hidden hand. Only a fool would come to such a meeting without having something at the ready.

After he had reached the top, the rider halted a few paces away from where Halsedric stood. Dark, suspicious eyes glared down from narrow lids as the rider lifted the once-hidden axe into his lap. He was as the Elanni had described him. The thin hairs sprouting from his jaw formed a poor and patchy beard. His frame was rugged and lean, made to endure the elements and the rigors of the wilds.

The horse snorted as Halsedric raised his hand in greeting. "Welcome, friend," he said to the man with a half-hearted smile.

The figure on the horse turned the beast slightly and looked Halsedric up and down. With tight blonde curls gracing his crown and fair skin, Halsedric seemed a picture of youth. Yet, as handsome and noble as he appeared, Halsedric's garb spoke differently. His cloak was worn at the fringes and was stained from years of travel. His boots still had patches of mud on them and there were traces of dirt on his fingers.

"What's under the cloak?" said the man on the horse, shifting the axe in his lap. His mount grumbled softly and twitched, sensing his owner's anxious and suspicious nature.

Lifting his left hand, Halsedric slowly opened the fringe of his cloak, exposing the hilt of his sword.

"Call me friend, yet you bring a sword?" said the stranger in a tense and forceful tone. "Speak quick, lessin' our time here be done."

Lowering the fringe of his cloak, Halsedric answered. "We have a mutual friend, you and I."

"Who?"

"Roe, is it?" asked Halsedric, his head tilting to one side as he spoke. His eyes squinted as the bright sun reigned down overhead.

"We are done here," brusquely answered the rider, pulling back on his reins. The horse responded by reluctantly lifting its head, grumbling, and stepping back a pace or two.

As Roe started to turn the horse, exposing the right flank of the beast, Halsedric called out, "A prophet named Wolland sent me. He asked that I relay a message to you."

"Don't know him. Don't care to," replied Roe as the horse came about. As he lifted the reins and lifted his feet to prod the horse forward, Halsedric cried out a name.

"Vellamilla!"

The horse started to move forward but soon halted as the trapper pulled back on the reins.

Roe's head snapped at once to stare at Halsedric again. Pulling out the axe from his lap and letting the weapon hang down at his side, he exclaimed, "What say you?"

"Vellamilla," answered Halsedric, this time with less urgency.

In response, Roe turned the horse about again, the beast nervously pacing into place, grumbling.

"Wolland, you say?" said Roe, those narrow eyes suddenly curious.

"You have a phrase to offer in reply," said Halsedric, this time his voice less friendly.

"How's the old codger?"

"Well enough," answered Halsedric as he pulled back the fringe of his cloak. The hilt of the blade was exposed—a decorative pommel fashioned in the bud of a rose, beneath which a hilt of gleaming white bone lay. "Now, if you would, the words of reply."

Roe gazed at the hilt of the sword briefly with the hint of a smile. "Aye. Somethin' about geese nestin' in the winter."

"Where?"

Roe's head bowed as he took a moment to remember something learned long ago, but never practiced. "That's it," he said in a murmur. "Geese don't nest in the Aranach come winter. Or somethin' like that."

As Roe brought his horse about again to face Halsedric, Halsedric turned his head to the left and let out a shrill whistle. When it turned back, he spoke to the trapper in a very casual manner. "Do not be alarmed."

Roe's brow furrowed, Halsedric's gaze being met with a smirk. "Alarmed? About what?"

It only took a moment before Roe looked to the other side. A diminutive form materialized out of the willows, seemingly out of thin air. It moved with a purposeful march directly toward the pair. One hand clasped the curved wood of a bow with two white-fletched arrows. The other pulled back the hood of a cloak to reveal a maiden of exquisite beauty. Her long golden mane was braided and bound behind her head, exposing much of her fair-complected skin in the bright spring sun. Yet, as striking as she was, the one feature that caught Roe's rapt attention was her eyes. For her eyes were as bright as blue sapphire and with a hue so intense that they almost seemed to glow.

Roe's horse snorted and started to stomp at the unexpected appearance of the maiden from the trees. He mumbled something indistinct as he struggled to control his mount.

"This is my companion, Herodiani," said Halsedric in an offhand way. "She will accompany us."

Behind her, also appearing out of the trees came three horses, each of them having a stunning silvery white quality to their coats. Two bore blankets of a dark greenish gray on their back with a third sporting a saddle of sorts with cross braces before and behind. From this, bags and packs were secured to it with a thin rope. None bore bridles or reins and had nothing to keep them from wandering or grazing. And while Herodiani approached Roe and his mount, the horses remained partially in the cover of the trees, seeming to hang back just before the cresting of the hill. As if they intentionally chose to remain out of sight of the village.

Roe's attention was divided, and he was stunned past the point of intelligible speech. With his beast finally under control, he got a better look at the petite maiden who stood near Halsedric. Her cloak was a drab green clasped with a bronze disc, the garment hiding the earthen clothes she wore beneath. On her feet, she wore a supple sort of boot whose color and fabric matched that of her cloak. Her delicate arms were covered by sleeves of linen, or so it appeared, both hands wearing long gloves of a chestnut hue to protect them from the rigors of the bow. Her sharp features, youthful appearance, and unexpected beauty both intrigued him and left him confused. This was a young maiden better suited for the halls of some lord's mansion, not the rough-and-tumble wilds.

Roe's unconscious stare was returned by Herodiani's scorching gaze, breaking the spell he was under.

"I assume you were informed of our arrival?" said Halsedric, taking Roe's attention away from the Elanni huntress.

Roe's answer was little more than a grunt and a nod. He followed with, "Didn't know who I'd be meetin' though."

Taking a moment to view the village in the distance, Halsedric noticed others were watching. Small forms among the disorderly array of buildings began to gather, their numbers having grown since Roe's approach.

"We should be away from here," said Halsedric, intently staring down at the village. "Do you have a camp nearby?"

"Been hole up at the Hale house, about a day's ride from here." He paused for a moment and looked up at the sky. "Well, a day's ride if'n I didn't have someone watchin' me all this time. Might need to make camp somewhere come nightfall."

Lifting his hand and motioning to Roe, Halsedric answered, "Very well. We will mount our horses, and—"

"It'll be a bit before we do, tho," Roe interrupted. "I need to go back for my things."

Halsedric's stare at the trapper said it all. Part confused and part annoyed, he may have understood the logic of the trapper leaving his things behind, but his concern started to grow. He wanted to be away from that place, and away from the spying eyes of the villagers that gathered in the distance.

"You didn't expect me to bring me things to a meetin' with a stranger, did you?"

Halsedric waved him off, his voice low and disappointed. "Go then, and be quick."

Roe pulled on the reins, prodding his horse with one foot and pointing the beast in the direction of the town. Before departing, he turned his head to Halsedric once more and spoke. "By the way, friend, two men were askin' the alewife about you, and who you was lookin' for. Overheard them on the way out."

His words went still for a time before he continued. "Make ready to go as soon as I round the hill. I want to be gone from here right quick if'n some decide to follow."

Clicking his tongue and digging his heels into the flanks of his mount, Roe prodded his horse forward. Halsedric and Herodiani watched passively as he departed, slowly at first, the beast struggling with the grade of the hill. When the trapper was well out of earshot, Herodiani drew close and spoke.

"Do you think anyone will follow?"

"Let us pray none do," answered Halsedric.

CHAPTER THREE

IN THE AMBER GLOW OF THEIR SMALL FIRE, ROE inspected the map that Halsedric provided. Fingers stained with dust and grime felt the edges of the document, noting the smooth feel and the weight of the paper upon which a map was drawn.

"Feels like hide," Roe remarked, sounding a little surprised. "Thinner, though."

To make reading it more manageable, Roe folded the map in half before he leaned closer to the firelight. His blanket lay out near the modest blaze, Roe sat cross-legged on what would be his bed for that evening. A spot that was close enough to be warm and far enough away to avoid the pop of embers. By the way he squinted, it was clear to Halsedric that the trapper was having difficulty reading the fine art and markings laid down by the Elanni mapmakers. It was a map the warrior had drawn up as he wintered over in the lands of Elenur, the details of it taken from a more ancient source.

"It is a special kind of parchment," Halsedric remarked. "Without the need for a hide." He paused for a moment as he studied Roe's expression. "Do you require a lamp?"

"Aye," answered Roe. He set aside the map and twisted about to his left where his gear was secured. Pointing to the stack of branches and stems they acquired earlier, he muttered, "Fetch me a stem to light it."

The lamp itself was made of brass with a ring for a handle that perforated a conical top. A hinged door allowed access to the wick, and a short tube extended out at an angle where the reservoir of oil could be refilled, stopped by a cork. It took time for Roe to get a branch lit from the fire. Most of the fuel that they gathered was from the willows that grew nearby—a tree whose limbs were not optimal for a fire. Luckily, the dead reeds left behind by the autumn of the year prior made for a fine tinder, allowing them to stoke the fire quickly.

When the wick was lit, Roe cast the twig back into the fire before closing the door, a simple clasp making a click as it pressed into place.

"Here, hold this if'n you would," Roe said as he held the lamp up by the ring. Halsedric knelt next to Roe and took the lamp offered to him. His hands free once more, Roe once again examined the map.

Pointing to the fine Elanni script along the features drawn on the map, Roe asked, "What's the meanin' of this?"

Halsedric leaned in, drawing the lamp closer to read the elegant script. Located next to an expanse of water connected north and south by a river course, he answered, "*Lela Pilandanoria.* 'Lake of the Mirrored Waters,' in the tongue of the Ageless. The course that runs through it is called the *Adennuae.*"

With his finger, Roe traced the line that marked the river's passing as it curved north and east. He stopped when it came to a series of markings that looked like towers, four in all, spaced across the terrain in a rough semi-circle whose arc faced westward. Further east, amidst a series of mounds that represented hills, a fifth tower rose, this being slightly larger than the others. Roe's finger tapped the spot. "And this?"

"My destination," said Halsedric. "One of the things I must accomplish in this realm."

"Aye, but what is it?"

"An ancient fortress," answered Halsedric. "A ruin now—"

"Aye," interrupted Roe. "I know of what you speak. The only question I got is why you'd want to go there?"

"It was the seat of an ancient king. A king we now know is very much alive."

Lowering the map, Roe turned his head slightly and gave Halsedric a sidelong look. "You mean, like them Elanni?"

"No," Halsedric answered quickly, shaking his head as he did. "This king was a mortal."

"Like a ghost then? Or real? Flesh and blood?"

Halsedric grimaced slightly. "More like a ghost. Though flesh and blood may not be long behind. Or a similar form. Perhaps one less...earthly."

Lifting the map once more, Roe remarked under his breath, "I ain't likin' the sound of that."

"Only of late have we become aware of a dark faith that has sprung up in hidden places," said Halsedric as Roe continued to study the map. "And, if what we discovered in the Aranach holds true, they have been engaged in their sinister activities for some time. It is my supposition that this king might return to his ancient home. He once ruled his dark kingdom from that holdfast. Reason compels me to investigate."

"Mayhaps it's a wise thing too," answered Roe. At once, his finger traced the arc of the four towers. "What's this, then?"

"A series of redoubts, I assume. A fence of fortifications where troops were housed and dispatched. In the war, the enemy invaded from the south and the east. Setting a ring of outer holdfasts might blunt or counter any westward thrust of an offensive against the main fortress."

"Well, there ain't much to return to," said Roe, folding the map in half. "I was asked to scout. Well, I scouted."

"And?"

"It's a ruin. Ain't much to go back to, if'n you ask me."

"What did you find within?"

"Nope," said Roe with a shake of his head. "I ain't that daft. I stopped before the gates...or what's left of them."

Halsedric shot the trapper an expectant look, compelling Roe to elaborate.

"An old road leads right up to it. Though as you might be suspectin', I went by diffn't paths to get there. The road comes to a bridge where a stream cuts through the forest."

"Forest?"

Unfolding the map, Roe's index finger moved in an elliptical fashion around the fifth tower. "This here? All trees. Been like that long before I came to these lands. I know a few folk who can tell you about it. And a few other things as well."

"Tell me more," said Halsedric.

Roe folded the map again before speaking. "Been talk for a long time about strange folk in these parts. Some of the folk hereabouts have stories. Hooded men hidin' out in their stables at night. Wanderers gatherin' corn at corners of their fields as the sundown comes. And, been folks gone missin'. A few here and there. Them homesteaders are a close lot. There might be bad blood between a few, but ain't none likely to snatch up others. 'Ceptin' a few, whom most folk here despise."

Roe paused before speaking. "Strangers ain't welcome in these parts, lessin' you're a merchant with wares in tow."

"Yes, so I have been told," interjected Halsedric.

"Been problems with raiders in the past," continued Roe. "Some think it's raiders come back again, but most say no. Them wanderers and the missin' folk has lessened some of late. But folk still ain't restin' so easy, if'n you hear my meanin'."

Unfolding the map once more, Roe pointed to a stream that cut across the region of hills where the fifth tower was placed. "The road I spoke of? It has a bridge over this stream here. Been repaired. You can see where new mortar and fresh-cut stone have been set. So, if there be travelers, mayhaps they be goin' by that road. Though, not sure why someone would want to visit them ruins. As much of a chill as they put up my back...still, ain't naught but busted down old stone."

"Believe me if you will," Halsedric answered him. "I say, with some authority, that such evil oft sets roots that run deep." A thought came to Halsedric’s mind. “So, were there any of these travelers at the ruins?”

“Can’t says I got too close to look,” answered Roe. “Seen tracks in the dirt and I heard what I reckoned were voices, but naught else.”

Head bowed, Halsedric pondered in silence. His concentration was broken as Roe spoke once more.

“Weren’t wantin’ to tarry too long in that place,” Roe said with a muted huff.

“What say you?”

“The trees,” he said in a voice that seemed bothered and befuddled. “They weren’t...natural, if you get my meanin’.”

“Not natural? In what way?”

Roe motioned in the air, map in one hand, the other hand with fingers curled. “Well, they was like—” After a short pause, Roe continued, but his words weren’t so certain. “Like they was once trees but made into somethin’ else.”

“Tell me more.” Halsedric was now intrigued, and those pale blue eyes bore down on the trapper with a cold determination.

For a time, Roe struggled with the words, but couldn’t properly describe what he witnessed. Letting his hands fall, he let slip a frustrated sigh. “If’n we’re goin’ there, you’ll see soon enough.”

“Is that all? Is that all you saw?”

“Well, there were these mounds. Barrows, I think. Lots of them,” Roe said. “Lost my bearin's once while I was in there. Made me near as wary as them gates of them ruins, the hair standin' up on the back of my neck and all."

Hearing this, Halsedric's stare grew more intense. "How many were there?"

"How many?" Roe snorted, a disbelieving smirk gracing his lips. "I weren't about ready to linger there and count. Not in that place." His grin fell, and he continued with a softer tone of voice. "I backtracked and made for the forest fringe ere nightfall. Figured I'd make camp, then strike out next day. `Twas early spring and the nights was still cold. I weren't about to make a fire, given where I was. So, I found me a fallen tree, made a bed with pine boughs, and covered it over with the same. And lucky I did."

Roe had Halsedric's rapt attention as he continued his tale. "Somethin' came followin' after. Followin' the trail I made." Then, Roe went silent, and his eyes glazed over in a faraway stare.

Halsedric waited for a short time, expecting Roe to continue. He quickly grew impatient. "And what did you see?"

"See?" Roe said, Halsedric breaking the trance he was in. "Twas night, friend. In the forest. Weren't nothin' *to* see. But I could hear them searchin' for a time before they wandered off. I swear, I didn't sleep at all that night. Headed back come dawn, knowin' I was found out. I waited a spell before I tried goin' back there again."

After a time, Roe handed back the map to Halsedric, the warrior exchanging the lamp for the document. Unfolding and folding the map once more along the original creases, Halsedric turned and picked up the oilcloth pouch that held it.

Roe watched as Halsedric threw back the long flap that covered the pouch's interior, then spoke. "On the morrow, I'll unload my things at Farmer Hale's, where I'm hole up for now. The day next, we can head out to speak with Gallain—"

"Who is this Gallain?"

"Farmer out on some of them lands closest to the Wychwood."

"Wychwood?" Halsedric said as he wrapped the flap about the pouch before flipping it over and tying the bundle closed. "Is that what the residents here call the forest?"

"Aye," answered Roe with a nod. "And from some of the stories they tell, and seein' it with my own eyes, I can say it's a right proper name for the place."

Roe watched Halsedric return the map to his bag. As Halsedric was retying the strap, Roe asked, "Why else have you come?"

"What say you?"

Roe hesitated before answering. With uncertain words, he said, "You said them ruins was just part of your mission. What else you need do?"

The shadows cast by the firelight made the features of Halsedric's distressed expression seem pained. As he returned to his place at the fire, he spoke. "You are not the only eyes we have in these parts."

"Oh?"

"Another there was," continued Halsedric. "One who has since gone missing."

"And whereabouts—"

"The City of Orem," interjected Halsedric, answering Roe's question before it could be completed. "These lands have a dark history. The fences of this nation encompass places once torn down and left desolate in ancient days. Peace may reign for an age. Yet, as I have already said, the stains of such evils are not easily removed. The cursed earth oft beckons evil from afar when the watchfulness of the righteous sleeps.

A dark sect has, for too long, toiled unseen. Only in recent years have we uncovered the worship of some hidden god or devil. One that has sent the unwary to their doom and has set about building an army of blasphemous creations. To what ends, I know naught. Much has been lost and forgotten in both the consequence of war and the passing of time. Thus, I must uncover and relearn those gaps in our understanding."

"And what's it you're seekin'?" asked Roe.

Once more, Halsedric looked pained. He inhaled noisily and sighed loudly in frustration.

"It is not what I seek. It is what I will find. For if I am to be sent to attend such things, it is certain that what troubles this place is far worse than travelers and raiders."

"Right," mumbled Roe as he opened the door of the lamp. The hinge creaked as the bent brass of the door swung outward. Puffing his cheeks, he blew hard into the interior, extinguishing the flame. A fragrant but dark and thready smoke rose from the holes in the side of the lamp. Setting it down, he looked away from Halsedric and the fire, seemingly dispassionate but preoccupied. The fire snapped and hissed as the gentle sound of a nearby stream accompanied it. These were the noises that filled the lull in the conversation, though not for long.

"Where's the maid?" Roe turned his head to look at Halsedric. Halsedric himself was sitting on his own blanket, his sword across his lap. Nearby, the horses milled about, Roe taking notice of the forms moving in the dark.

"She is on watch," answered Halsedric calmly.

"And who's next to keep watch?"

"None."

"None?" Roe's tone reflected his disbelief.

"The Elanni have no need for sleep, and their eyes are not blind as those of men beneath moon and stars. This is why she accompanies me on such treks."

A horse snorted, and Roe's head turned quickly to one side, looking at the vague shapes moving just beyond the reach of the firelight.

As if sensing the trapper's anxiety, Halsedric spoke to him in a calm and knowing voice. "You need not fear. Our mounts will tend to your beasts."

"You sure?" Roe's disbelief was tinged with concern.

Turning his head with a knowing expression in his eyes, Halsedric replied, "Your beasts would not be the first they have shepherded. Be at peace. They will be there come the dawn."

"Right, right," said Roe with a nod and low voice, the sound of it not as sure as the words. There was another lull, and then he spoke again. "Where'd you meet her?"

"Herodiani?"

"Aye," acknowledged Roe, his eyes on the fire.

"Many years ago. The second time I wintered in the Kingdom of Elenur. Her father was gracious enough to house me for the winter months."

Roe turned his head and looked at Halsedric directly. He went to speak, then suddenly turned shy, downcast eyes hinting at reluctance. When he did finally muster the words, he mumbled, his words halting and uncertain. "You two—" His hands waved about in a confused dance, reflecting his troubled mind. "You two...are you...?"

"No," answered Halsedric with a sidelong look, almost sounding annoyed. "She is a valued companion and kindred heart. She has been with me on many of my travels, and I greatly value her dedication, skill, and cunning." The sidelong look then turned into a full, irksome glare. "That is all."

"Aye, right," Roe muttered shamefaced.

But Halsedric wasn't done. With a hint of steel in his voice, he continued addressing the trapper. "Nor should you entertain even a single thought that she is anything other than a companion and ally. Understood?"

It took Roe a moment to answer, and when he did, it was a nod and a grunt.

As Halsedric lifted his intimidating stare and returned to gazing at the fire, he added, "She has lived hundreds of years. You are naught but a babe in her eyes."

"Hundreds?" Roe's head lifted, surprised. "She looks like a young maid."

"And so she shall, long after our bones are dust. Lest misfortune find her."

"Misfortune?"

The fire's light bathed Halsedric's face with an orange glow and shadows as the fire popped. Something inside the low blaze let out a long stuttering hiss. What distress Halsedric tried to conceal, the light of the flames seemed to betray. From the ground, he took a stray fragment of a dead reed and rolled it between his fingers. "Misfortune haunts her. I speak of

Lord Aurogeloi as if he were her father, yet he is her foster-father. She was but a young child during the years of the Great War. He had lost his family; she, hers. So, it was he who took her into his house and raised her as his own when the war was concluded. Ever does her loss tear at her heart. She offers aid in my endeavors. As if it may somehow undo the hurts she has suffered."

Casting the fragment of reed into the fire, he turned to face Roe. Those pale eyes stared hard, being both serious and sad. "I am as I am, as I was remade by the Allfather. To face and overcome great peril. She has naught but her skill and wit. While you may see her as a youthful maid, perhaps in the first bloom of her feminine form, it is a mask. A ruse. A pleasant deception that hides a skilled and deadly huntress and warrior."

Roe took a moment to gaze upon those serious pale eyes, pondering their meaning in the protracted silence that followed. As Halsedric turned away once more, Roe spoke. "If'n she's as good as you say, why the worry?"

"Even the most skilled may stumble," answered Halsedric.

CHAPTER FOUR

It was not much further to the homestead of Farmer Hale. Most of the farms in this region consisted of several familial dwellings centered around a communal well, the largest of the homes being where the patriarch resided. In and around the lodgings, several outbuildings were often raised. Stables and a barn. Housing for hens and pens for goats and pigs. Then there were small huts where meat could be aged, along with one or more granaries where the year's harvest was stowed. The estate of Farmer Hale had all of these, though, by all accounts, his enterprise was larger and more established than most in the region. His was a multi-generational farm that had grown over unnumbered years of plenty and strife. The secondary dwellings that dotted the area where sons and brothers resided with their families, the walls formed from wattle and daub set in a low stone foundation. The granaries were built with bricks of clay and dung, baked in the sun until they were hard as stone. The rest were constructed of packed sod or compressed dirt that was just as dense and firm. What little wood existed in the varying structures dotting the landscape was used to erect peaked roofs that were covered with thatch. Long eaves extended far past the walls as was common in the region. Where the eaves ended, stone-lined ditches ran, which emptied into buried cisterns used to capture the rainfall.

None of these were as extensive as the main house, where Farmer Hale resided. Constructed of fieldstone and mortar, it had an attached pen where heifers were housed. Longer than it was wide, it contained several chimneys where fires were used to heat the interior as well as cook in the winter months. Expanded over numerous generations of Hale's ancestors, the main home was as majestic as one might find here in this far-flung agrarian countryside.

Right outside the long stone house, near the front entry, was an open structure with low walls made of mounded earth that were packed hard and covered with grass. The large round oven with a stone chimney made it clear this was an outdoor kitchen where food was prepared in the warmer seasons. While the noontime meal had already passed, the kitchen was still abuzz with activity. For there was still much to do to make ready the evening meal.

As the trio approached this rustic estate, they rode past vast fields where the spring wheat was sprouting. Long rectangular plots where green stalks grew in militaristic order stretched for some distance from the main home, and beyond. Other plots were still being tilled, horses and plows engaged to turn over the dirt, each team under the care of one of the farmer's sons and their kin. It was a place that was active, bustling, and filled with life, despite its vast scope.

Roe led them past the people working in the fields to the main house, as the great hounds of the homestead approached and barked their warnings. These Roe ignored, turning back to the others as they slowed. "Don't fret about them much. They'll only come at you if'n Hale tells them to."

Eventually, their trail led them to a barn where Roe had taken up residence. It wasn't much, the walls being made of hardened sod. Yet, it was high enough that a wooden loft was erected so that additional hay could be stored high. Other mounds of dried grasses filled the interior, though it was clear much of what was once stored here had been removed to feed the grazing animals during winter. Here the trio dismounted as one of the large white dogs drew near.

The horses milled about as Roe unloaded his things into the interior of the barn. As he did, he managed a closer look at the horses Halsedric and Herodiani rode, his hands stroking the soft flanks of the creatures.

"Beautiful beasts," remarked Roe of the Lenogala. The horses remained close to their riders despite having no saddle or bridle.

One of the silvery-white creatures snorted, seemingly in reply.

"Areosindew offers you his gratitude for your kind words," Herodiani said, as if interpreting the noise the horse made. The remark left the trapper with a befuddled expression on his face.

Not long after, Farmer Hale, the patriarch of the familial estate, approached and offered his greetings. He was a wiry man, his skin like that of tanned leather, having spent decades tending the fields beneath the open sun. Clean-shaven, he had a rounded face and chin, his lips and smile having a sort of rubbery and expressive nature. When the man smiled, his lips seemed to stretch from ear to ear. Yet, when he was serious, his countenance could be hard and his eyes threatening. Attending him was one of his sons, both men dressed in garb that was almost a uniform for the region. The clothes were typically made from thread that was unbleached and undyed, the weave of the fabric having earthen tones. While most of the men who tended the fields sported vests either of leather or wool, Farmer Hale wore only his baggy shirt of linen. A garment that was well-used, stained, and patched at the elbows. His sleeves were rolled up, and the opening of the garment was left untied at the top due to the growing heat of the day. Cotton trousers were held up by a belt of weathered and stained leather cinched about his waist, his shirt tucked beneath. Yet what stood out about him, and the menfolk of that region, was their tall boots. Firm soles made of wood and hide were stitched to long shafts of leather that ended just below the knees, the two halves separated by a long tongue. Over these, crisscrossed laces of leather wound around metal hooks riveted into the boots, pulled tight, and held fast by a bow at the top. Into these were tucked the legs of their trousers in order to protect them from being torn and stained while they labored.

Atop Hale's head was a woven hat of straw that hid his bald crown. Short black hair peeked out beneath the brim, the last vestiges of his youthful mane now flecked with gray. As was common in the region, the hat had a wide brim, shielding the face of its wearer from the punishing sun that shone down from above.

"Who's this, then, come to my 'stead?" shouted Farmer Hale as he approached. His face looked stern as his eyes fixed on the trapper.

"Friends!" shouted Roe in reply. His answer seemed to soften the farmer's demeanor, the concern fading from Hale's expression soon after.

Slowing his approach, the farmer took notice of the Lenogala horses, remarking, "Fine beasts you got there."

Halsedric stepped forward to greet the farmer, a shallow bow signaling his respect and appreciation for the aging patriarch. "Your hospitality is greatly appreciated."

"Aww, ain't nothin'," answered the farmer with a wave of his hand. "Any friend of Roe here is a friend of mine!"

"We'll be off to the home of Gallain come mornin'," said Roe, removing the saddle from his horse as he spoke.

Hands on his hips, Farmer Hale nodded and smiled. "Well, as I saids before, friends of Roe is friends of ours. He's been a mighty big help in these parts with them fox and stag and all." He looked about, surveying the homestead. "Ain't got much room here. Not sure what you'll do with your beasts. We've got some hay to spare if'n you need it…for the beasts, that is." He stopped and chuckled. "If'n there be one thing we got out here, it's hay.

And a couple of you is welcome to stay in the house if'n you wants." The farmer's head tilted upwards as he looked at the sky. "Gonna be dry today an' the next. Tho' weather changes quick in these parts."

"Any space to lay our heads is greatly appreciated," answered Halsedric with a shallow grin. "I think we will be fine among the hay. You need not worry about our mounts. They will be fine and will not wander."

"Suits yourself," answered the farmer. "But I have's to warn you—if'n your beasts go wanderin' off, we here ain't gonna run after 'em."

"Fair enough."

Farmer Hale pointed to a pit lined with stone some distance toward the house and away from the barn. "That there's the burn pit, if'n you want a fire to chase away the night. There's some wood and dung around the side of the house. Make sure you close the door on the barn and keep the fire low. Don't need my barn burnin' down, if'n you know what I mean."

"As you wish," answered Halsedric with a nod. It was then that Herodiani passed behind him as she made toward the barn. Hood down and head bowed, she did her best to prevent others from getting a good look at her features.

"A bit late for the noontime meal. If'n you're wantin', come supper, I'll bring some stew 'round for you and yours and—"

Hale noticed the passing of the huntress. His speech stalled for a moment as he eyed her. His awkward expression made it clear he was trying to appear as if he was less curious about the Elanni maid than he actually was. Soon after, he removed his cap briefly as he wiped his crown with his hand. His brows creased as he returned the hat to his head. In a voice just above a whisper, he said, "That be a woman?"

The slight smile that graced Halsedric's face fell in expectation of an unwelcome explanation. He stepped forward and bent down slightly so as to talk to the farmer with a certain measure of privacy. "Indeed," he said in a low voice. "Her name is Herodiani."

"Your woman?"

"Not...exactly," Halsedric answered. "She is a huntress, and quite skilled with both bow and sword." He paused for a moment and turned his eyes to the distracted farmer. "And, if I may say, she can have a rather irascible temperament."

His head turning with a snap to face Halsedric, the farmer offered a look that echoed his perplexity. "Ir...irrace—"

"She angers quite easily."

Mouth open, the Farmer's head went back, understanding now what Halsedric was trying to say. "Why didn't you says so, then? Right, then! I can't do much for the hounds, but they ain't goin' to be much bother, save for a sniff or two. Mayhaps lookin' for a morsel to eat. But, I'll tell the boys to steer clear and keep them eyes to themselves."

"That would be greatly appreciated," replied Halsedric with a slow grin.

"And if the hounds be much of a bother, tell her don't kills 'em!" said Farmer Hale, nervous. With a sidelong look at the barn, he added, "We need 'em 'round here."

The grin grew on Halsedric's face. "I will inform her of their importance."

"Thank'ee," nodded the farmer with that broad smile of his. He started to turn and leave, then paused. "And don't forget, I'll be bringin' supper 'round some time after dusk."

"Your hospitality is much appreciated, good sir."

Hale nodded again and raised his hand in the air briefly. Whether it was a wave, or a signal to someone else, Halsedric was unable to tell. Though he did feel the palpable concern the farmer felt, worried that in offering a place for the night, he had invited trouble to his household. Halsedric watched Hale depart for a moment before he started to make his way back to the barn.

The night came in its own time, both Roe and Halsedric leaving the confines of the barn to fetch fuel and build a fire before the dark descended. As dusk had neared its end, Farmer Hale appeared out from the confines of the outdoor kitchen. The rest of the family having returned to their various homes, the voices of the children and workers were now distant or silent. A chorus of night bugs arose, their collective song contesting with the sound of burning wood, the occasional bleating of a goat, or the grunt of a sow. A stray fly buzzed by the fire, the area surprisingly free of midges and other such nuisances, the ground being mostly dirt. The scent of smoke and hay predominated at times, along with the heady musk of the hounds who lay nearby, detectable when the breeze was right.

In Farmer Hale's hands was a plank of wood, whereupon three loaves were placed, the tops torn away. From each loaf, thin ghostly ribbons of steam rose from something dark within the center, some of the contents having run down the sides of the bready mounds when ladled from the pot.

"Ho there!" The farmer greeted them, his attention solely focused on the three loaves. "I got's supper for you. I'm hopin' you like stew."

Stew was a common fare in the rural outlands, a recipe that varied from tavern to tavern, house to house. It could be a delight, if made well, or barely edible at its worst. The thick brown broth of this variation was a far sight from the elegant fare of the Elanni. Yet, it was an improvement over the travel cakes and dried meat they had been consuming on their trek to the Orem.

As Farmer Hale rounded the gathering, he bent down. Each of the trio rose and took their respective loaves from the plank. Soon after, the farmer withdrew, taking his platter with him. In the time it took Halsedric to gather a spoon from his gear, the farmer returned juggling three stools, a long-stemmed pipe, and a leathery pouch Halsedric assumed to contain pipeweed. Setting two of the stools down in front of him, he positioned the third seat behind him and sat.

After Herodiani took one of the stools, Hale opened the pouch and stuffed two fingers inside. Pinched between the calloused digits of the farmer was a wad of dark tobacco fragments. Stuffing the chopped and fermented weed into the clay bowl of his pipe, he tamped down the wad into the space with his small finger. Shifting to one side, he pulled a bent branch from his pocket. Thereafter, he lifted himself from his seat and stuck one end into the flames until it caught fire. While the others went about consuming their meal, he gingerly withdrew the branch, trying his best to not extinguish the infant tongue of flame that clung to the end. Slowly settling onto his stool, he lit the bowl of his pipe. After several draws, a thin stream of smoke started to issue from his lips. Between draws, the farmer spoke. "We don't get many visitin' out here. I might say, your comin' made for a bit o' excitement." His words ended with a subtle laugh.

After chewing and swallowing, Halsedric answered, "We are eternally grateful for your hospitality, good sir."

"Aw, don't think nothin' `bout it," answered the farmer, flapping the twig in the air to extinguish the flame. He drew on his pipe once more and let out a large cloud of smoke that danced before dissipating in the night's gentle breeze. "We're simple folk out heres. Most hereabouts are kindly. Plus, a fightin' man such as yourself is a goodly thing to have `bout in these days."

"What say you?" Herodiani spoke up.

Hale turned to look at the Elanni maid. While her beauty may have caught his attention, it was her stunning eyes upon which his gaze was fixed. Hale's mouth opened a bit, rather dumbstruck by the sight.

Roe broke this brief and awkward pause by clearing his throat. "Aye," he said loudly, the words breaking the spell the farmer was under. "Missin' folk and wanderin' types. I spoke of them earlier."

"Have you had such troubles?" asked Halsedric as he lifted a spoonful of stew from the bowl before shoveling it into his mouth.

It took the farmer a moment to collect his thoughts. "Troubles? Aye." The farmer nodded as he spoke, sitting forward and cradling the bowl of the pipe in his ruddy hands. "Been strange folk sneakin' `bout. And we's been hearin' tales told of folk gone missin' in the night. They say it used to be worse long ago when there were troubles aplenty." Taking up the stem of his pipe, he twisted about and behind, using the stem to point ahead, somewhere in the distance. "Used to be lands and homesteads well past here, all the way to the West Bramble. First, it was the raiders. Drove most folk off their lands, fleein' west."

Hale took another draw on his pipe. The wind gusted slightly as he pulled the smoke through the stem and steadily exhaled it in a plume. "The raidin' has stopped, but ain't no one wanting to stretch further out where we's are. Them lands would still be empty, if'n it weren't for some of them herdfolk and their flocks. And the stories they tell?" Farmer Hale let out a piercing whistle from his pursed lips. "Sons and daughters gone missin'. Dead hounds. Filched herds. Dark folk moving in the night."

"Aye," nodded Roe as he interjected. His words were uncouth and muffled as he spoke with a mouth full of bread and stew. "Most of them lords in the city have been telling the herdfolk to move their flocks closer to the villages and farmsteads with all the poachin' goin' on."

"Yep," agreed the farmer. "Most of the land in these parts be leased. Only a few of the farmfolk hereabouts tendin' their own land. Them sheep of the herdfolk don't care if'n they eat grass or corn from leasefolk or free, tended land or wild. Causin' bad blood, it is." Taking another draw of his pipe, the smoke escaped his lips as he continued talking. "We trade with them herdfolk from time to time. I ain't got no grief with most. A few of 'em don't keep their herd as good as they should, and they tend to let 'em wander. Them I chase off.

Still, I've been tryin' to get some of them landed folk in Orem to let slip a few of that mound of coin they horde, to buy a few posts, so's I can put up some fencin' an' whatnot.

Seein' it's their herds been eatin' my crops." Hale ended with a disaffected grumble

"What more do you know of these 'poachers,' as you call them?" asked Halsedric, setting his spoon in his bowl of bread.

"Nothin' much," answered the farmer, "save what I hears from the herdfolk."

"Are there no sheriffs?" inquired Herodiani, taking advantage of a short lull in the conversation.

"Aye," said Roe, wiping his mouth with his sleeve. His words were muffled and imprecise as he continued to chew his stew while he talked. "There's marshals hereabouts to keep the peace and such. Don't seem to be doin' much."

"Bah!" Farmer Hale waved his hand angrily and spat on the ground. "Them marshals! Always three days late, and beggin' a free meal for all their trouble," he said with drenching sarcasm. "What raiders they caught weren't naught but luck, I tells you! The only thing I can say `bout them that was good, is they was less useless before that Karne wormed his way into the Orem council." He paused for a moment staring at the ground, his wizened eyes kindled with the youthful flame of an angry man, his expressive face pinched in exasperation. "Gold over good, says I! Don't take no heart nor faith nowadays to make your way in the world. Jus' a few chests filled with silver, and the world be yours. Well, we've had many a petty lord wantin' to grow their house in the past. We didn't take their gold then. We ain't takin' *his* gold now!" He spat once more before muttering some unintelligible curse beneath his breath.

"Karne?" said Herodiani.

"Aye," said Roe with a nod, his eyes studiously avoiding hers. "Came to the city of Orem not long ago, he did. From the north, they say, with a rabble of northfolk with him."

This revelation immediately got Halsedric's attention. "North?"

"Aye." Farmer Hale pointed a finger at Halsedric. "Look like you, from what I hears. Gold hair. Blue eyes. Nolan, some say. Maybe horsefolk."

At once, Herodiani and Halsedric glanced at one another, each with a hint of surprise in their stare.

Roe continued the tale. "Bought up the debts of young Lord Aelbrech from what I hears. Assumed his house and holdin's."

"Been pushin' folk hereabouts to sell their land," the farmer quickly followed. "Offerin' thrice what most them petty lord types in Orem paid in the past. Some take the gold an' live on the lease. There be a few like me that tells them what they can do with their gold! No fool spends gold like that, lessin' there's something smellin' all foul behind it. And I ain't wantin' no part of that!" Using the stem of the pipe, he pointed at Halsedric. Through squinted eyes, he added, "My kin been farmin' these lands for longer than my mammy can remember. It's in the blood. And I ain't gonna shame my dear, dead pappy for a handful of shiny coins!" Then with a singular defiant motion, he placed the tip of the pipe between his teeth and bit down.

Yet, while Farmer Hale made his statement, Roe carefully spied the expressions of both Halsedric and Herodiani. When the farmer completed his rant, the trapper spoke up. "You know this Karne?"

Halsedric was guarded, and his expression reflected this. His reluctance to answer the question was seen in the lingering pause after the question that was posed. "We are aware of such a man, though not by that name."

With a laugh both brief and loud, the farmer's hand reached up, his fingers wrapping about the bowl of his pipe. "Don't surprise me none, seein' the company he keeps. Met a few of his creatures in the past. Like snakes 'neath the hay, they was."

His stare alternating between Roe and their host, Halsedric inquired, "What else can you tell me of this Karne?"

"Can't says I had the wont to know such a man overmuch, if'n you know what I means," Hale answered.

Roe was quick to follow. "Well, I know this—after Karne overtook the House of Aelbrech, he let go all the servants and brought in his own men. I was in an alehouse down in Orem when one of them was cryin' about his woes, deep into his drink. Let them go, every one. Some been tied to that house for generations."

"The Aelbrech been landed lords in these parts longer than most can remember," added Hale after taking another draw from his pipe. "Used to own land all the way east, even them places most good folk don't go. Not that it does 'em any good havin' land no one wants to tend."

Roe continued his report. "Weren't no secret young Lord Aelbrech had many debts and few means to pay them. Don't know if'n it was like that before he took his seat or after. I ain't no lord, so I ain't altogether sure. Most of them lords in the city have their lands and people on them. Maybe a bad crop one year, or one too many poor catches from the boats? Ain't sure. Though I'm sure havin' to spend gold for more marshals don't help much. And word has it, young Lord Aelbrech liked his games."

"Gambling?" inquired Halsedric.

"Aye," nodded Roe.

"Them lands far out? Homesteads like Gallain? Them's used to be owned by the House of Aelbrech since long before the city had walls. Lost most of them over time. Those they kept? Now they's owned by the House of Karne."

"And what became of this Lord Aelbrech?" inquired Halsedric.

A dread silence fell over the gathering. In time, Roe spoke up. "Don't know. I heard tales he was about in the city, but no one speaks of him no more. Strange doings if'n you ask me.

And, he had this manservant who ain't been seen nor heard from in some time."

Looking at Roe, Halsedric was pointed in his questioning. "How does a trapper know these things? Out here, far from the city?"

"Pelts," answered Roe with a mysterious grin, pulling away a piece of his bread.

"Pelts?"

"Aye," Roe answered as his teeth cut through the hard crust of the bread and tore away the remains. The rest of his explanation was broken at best, as he consumed his meal. "Most of them hides I have? I'll trade at the homes and villages. Fox. Stagskin. A wolf pelt or two. But some of them, mostly water game, furriers in the city will pay good coin, bein' in service to wealthy folk and such. And, in them Orem alehouses, there's all manner of folk and all manner of talk. Merchants. Soldiers. Potters. Even a noble princeling or two wantin' a little taste what common folk have."

"You ain't getting' them sorts of pelts out 'round these parts," remarked Farmer Hale.

Swallowing his bite, Roe answered, "Oh, I know places where they can be found." With a wink and a smile, he added, "And I keeps them to myself."

There was a sudden lull in the conversation. Farmer Hale continued to puff contently on his pipe while the others ate. Though brief, he'd cast an inquisitive glance at Herodiani. The mystery of her presence and the curiosity of her eyes had a hold on the old man.

After a time, he rose and addressed the others. "Well, now, I'd best be oft. I'll have one of the boys come `round with a bucket of water. You know where the well is if'n you need a drink or such. Quench the fire before you head off to sleep. And no fire in the barn, lessin' you want to be reapin' in the sun to replace it. And if'n trouble come in the night, call out."

Halsedric and Herodiani rose and bowed, thanking the farmer for his hospitality. When he departed, they sat once more, watching him disappear into the gathering night.

Roe watched Farmer Hale for a long time. Once assured he was out of earshot, he spoke to Halsedric in a grumbling tone. "Do you always ask your spies where they hear what they hear in front of strangers? Or is it just me?"

It took Halsedric a moment before he was able to ascertain what Roe was asking. He went to speak, but Roe was quick to cut him off. "If'n you want eyes and ears hereabouts, best to not ask too much. Even kindly tongues waggle when the ale flows. And if half of what I've heard said about Karne and his lot be true, there'll be one more missing spy hereabouts. Aye?"

It took Halsedric a moment to answer. Cradling the empty bowl of bread he responded, "Understood." He then turned to Roe and asked, "What do you think became of Lord Aelbrech?"

“Dead.” Roe’s tone was very cold as he cast a chunk of his bread at the hounds who waited in the near dark at the fringe of the fire. “Him and his manservant.”

CHAPTER FIVE

IT WAS A GENTLE SHOVE THAT WOKE HALSEDRIC in the middle of the night. Propped up against a pile of hay, a blanket separated him from the straw he rested against, his worn cloak covering his frame. His eyes opened with a snap in the darkness of the barn. At once, his head turned and his eyes followed the source of the disturbance. A vague form in shadows spoke to him in a voice soft and low.

"Visitors," Herodiani said.

"How many?"

"Six," she answered before she moved away.

Swiftly, Halsedric rose from his bed. As he did, his hand reached out and took hold of his sword. He could hear Herodiani rouse Roe somewhere in the darkness next to him

Lifting from the ground, Halsedric approached the entrance of the barn where they had been sleeping. Clutching the scabbard of his weapon with one hand, he inched his head past the opening to get a glimpse of what approached in the night.

Behind him, Halsedric heard Roe exclaim, "What?"

"Silence," Herodiani answered with a hiss. "Visitors approach."

Momentarily distracted by the sigh and shuffle of hay as Roe rose to his feet, Halsedric turned his attentions to the night's sky. The light of the half-moon was pale, and a great river of stars shone overhead. Were he one of the Elanni, the clear night might have aided him in assessing the gravity of the situation. That one gift, however, was not granted to him when he was revived from death's slumber long ago.

As he returned to spying the terrain past the homestead, he let the periphery of his vision aid him. Standing still, he patiently waited for the grainy and indistinct features of the undulating hills to reveal themselves, in spite of the night's shadow. His mind strained to interpret and identify even the most indistinct details or motions.

Then, he saw it. A pinprick of light. A momentary glimmer in the shadowy world beyond. A brief flash, and then gone. With it, he spied forms. Blobs of black against black, barely detectable as they moved and vanished at the crest of a nearby hill.

"Three gather at the south," Halsedric heard Herodiani say. Her footsteps were barely a whisper as she approached. "Three others gather at the west."

"I do not hear the hounds," remarked Halsedric as his neck craned back and around.

"Neither did I catch their scent," she answered. "They are downwind."

"Six, you say?"

"Yes."

"Where are the Lenogala?"

"I ordered them to move between the main house and the other dwellings," answered Herodiani. "I could—"

"No," interrupted Halsedric. "I do not think their assistance is required."

"What would you have me do?" whispered Roe, who also approached.

Halsedric pondered for a moment, twisting slightly. His eyes sought the fire that burned only a few hours before, forgetting it had been doused. He considered his options.

"I could take the three who approach from the west," offered Herodiani.

"I'll go with the maid," muttered Roe.

"No," Halsedric answered, addressing Roe with a measure of urgency. "You are our guide. Better you remain deep in the shadows. Find a place to hide, lest they come for you."

Roe started to speak, but Halsedric cut him off quickly. "There will be a time when valor will be required of you. This is not that hour. Now, withdraw if you please."

Halsedric turned away from Roe, whispering, "I do not think they come for you, but us. The huntress and I." Roe did not immediately withdraw, remaining instead to listen to the others devise their plans for the coming assault.

Motioning to Herodiani, Halsedric said, "Move out and around those that come from the west." He paused for a moment, turning at once to the entrance of the barn. "I will attend to our 'friends' at the south."

"Wound or slay?" whispered Herodiani.

Halsedric was quiet for a moment. "Slay them if they persist and be resolute in your attack." Pointing to the main house, he added, "There are lives other than our own that we must consider. Take what you need and go."

In the dark, Herodiani collected her things as Halsedric turned once more to Roe. Seeing his hazy form in the darkness, he rebuked the trapper. "Did I not say withdraw? Do so now."

As Roe slowly turned to find a hiding place within the barn, Halsedric returned to the entrance once more. "I have no desire to lose another spy in these lands."

Herodiani seemed to melt into the darkness as she exited the structure. After she departed, Halsedric returned to his place at the edge of the entrance, inching his head out past the edge of the doorway once more to keep watch. There, he fixed his gaze on the dark forms in the distance, his eyes straining to focus on the movement of indistinct shapes.

A goat bleated nearby, perhaps awakened by the activity in the barn. Or not. These things were difficult to discern. A dim light flashed and danced on the horizon, a sure sign of obvious movement. The night was oddly still, save for a gentle breeze that came and went. Like a ghost passing through to some unknown destination, a gentle wind ruffled the nearby hay.

As he waited, Halsedric pondered his options. Should he draw his sword? Should he commit the steely vengeance of the Allfather to such a fight? Or should the weapon remain resting in its sheath? Taking a mortal life was never an easy decision, especially in moments such as these. The blade was reserved for those things beyond the natural.

Withdrawing for a moment, he took hold of the hilt of his weapon and slowly withdrew the blade, wondering to himself if it might roar to life. With a slow, agonizing draw, he kept his eye on the blade, fearing not only the noise it might make, but the danger it presented to combustible hay stored within the shelter. He held his breath, waiting for the tip to slide free of the brass of the scabbard, swiftly holding the blade upright. Then he paused, nervously eyeing the weapon.

Nothing. Not even a dull red glow in the steel. He let the breath escape from his lips as he quickly moved to clear a spot on the dirt floor of the barn with his foot. Casting the empty sheath into the hay, he thrust the tip of his weapon into the dirt, leaving the blade to stand erect on its own. Having both hands free now, he could grapple with the coming foe, leaving his sword at the ready should the situation become dire. He returned again to the edge of the doorway and waited.

The light of a lamp drew near—the vague orange glow of the flame inside its holder. The furthest arc of the light crept forward along the ground, just at the fringe of his sight, where it halted. There it remained for a time, no doubt, as the mysterious lurkers assembled for their task.

Eyes closed, Halsedric listened intently in the dark. The ruffling of cloth and the shuffling of feet against hard earth sounded out. He heard the weak creak of metal against metal, no doubt, as the brass of the lamp swung on whatever holder it hung.

Then came the voices. "What if they're in the house?" whispered one. The sound was muffled slightly, the words difficult to understand. Halsedric assumed these nocturnal visitors wore coverings over their faces.

"We check the barn first," answered the other. "If they're not there, then the house."

There was a pause, and then the same voice spoke again. "You! Check for the others."

Hearing this, Halsedric slid back from where he stood, moving as quietly as he could to a spot in the center of the interior. Taking a position between the approaching men and Roe who hid somewhere behind, he made sure his sword was at least within the distance of a step or two should he need it. Then, arms out, every muscle tensed, he waited for their stalkers to reveal themselves.

Something moved in the space beyond the barn. A low form crouched, moving slowly, skulking in the black. A goat bleated in the distance, as did another. Halsedric fixed his gaze on the figure as it passed beyond the barn door, the gloom of the night concealing its form. Quietly, a thousand different scenarios and solutions passed through Halsedric's mind as he pondered what might happen next.

The form halted, standing erect, the light of a hidden lamp revealing the details of what approached. It was a man who was hooded and shrouded by a dark cloak. In one hand he held what looked to be a club. In the other, something drooped and dangled—a length of rope, as best as Halsedric could tell. The figure stood there for a moment staring into the black expanse of the structure's interior before lifting his club, motioning for his comrades to approach. Soon, two others emerged, one of them holding a brass lamp with a conical top.

The lamp dangled, suspended from a ring. A third form was like that of the first, who also carried both a rope and a cudgel. Halsedric did not need to guess as to the purpose of those clubs and cords.

The man with the lamp held it high to illuminate the interior. As the device cast its glow, it revealed to Halsedric the dark cloth mask that covered the face of the holder. Standing now in a line, each man varied in height, though there was one who stood taller than Halsedric.

As the light reached into the barn, it revealed Halsedric amidst the gloom. Seeing the warrior there in the middle of the barn, the man with the lamp spoke. Despite being muffled by the cloth that covered his face, his voice had a low and gruff quality to it. "That's one of 'em. Take him. And don't kill him. We want him alive. And the trapper, if he's in there."

The two men flanking the bearer of the lamp moved forward and then arced around, looking to come at Halsedric from the flanks. The warrior took a fighting stance, legs out, arms tensed to grapple. Determined eyes alternated between the two moving assailants as they neared, their clubs raised. Their strides were purposeful but leery. Too cautious, it seemed, for the man with the lamp. "Quickly, before we are noticed!"

The sound of a hound barking and the bleating of goats said otherwise. While others might be sleeping, the animals of the yard had already noticed the unwelcome guests in their midst.

Soon after, the man to Halsedric's right gave the warrior a warning. From behind his dark mask spoke a voice both thin and sinister. "Easy, now. Don't make us have to hurt you."

Halsedric's answer was cold silence and a stare as hard as flint. Both men dropped the ropes they carried in order to free their hands. As the reach of their fingers drew closer, Halsedric's fists clenched. Then, in an instant, the men closed and grappled with the warrior to subdue him.

Their attempts were vain and feeble, both men outmatched in strength, speed, and experience. The tangle of bodies, limbs, and cloth was a mess of grasping fingers, wrapping limbs, grunts, and curses. In the melee, Halsedric's attackers learned all too quickly that holding their intended victim was a task far more difficult than they had assumed.

At first, the one to the right tried to kick one of Halsedric's legs out from beneath him. Each attempt made was in vain, the warrior immobile and unfazed. The other laid a blow to the base of Halsedric's neck with his club. Whether intentional or poorly aimed, it was enough to cause a light to flash behind Halsedric's eyes, the world turning blurry after that. That's when the warrior finally retaliated.

The man to Halsedric's left was cast away like a rag doll, the attacker lifted high as he vaulted over the ground. When his feet finally made contact with the earth, he stumbled and fell back, finally landing in a mound of hay.

A worse fate befell the second attacker, for he received the full brunt of the warrior's wrath. One arm freed, Halsedric reached around and grabbed the man by one shoulder. With unnatural stealth and speed, the warrior broke away from the grasp of his assailant before pivoting and reaching into the hollow beneath the man's arm. Using his abnormal strength, Halsedric then lifted the man into the air, as if he were little more than a sack of grain, before casting him away. His feet scraping the ground, the man landed some feet away, stumbling at first. Having lost his footing, the hooded man flew back, his head slamming hard against the wooden post at the left side of the barn entrance. There was a muted crack and crunch as the back of the man's head hammered the post, the body crumpling to the ground.

By this time, the first attacker swiftly scrambled to his feet. His club raised in the air, the masked foe let out a guttural snarl as he charged the warrior.

Halsedric pivoted to face him. There was an attempt to brain Halsedric with the weapon, the cudgel coming down directly at Halsedric's head. Reaching up swiftly, the warrior took hold of the club midflight, stalling the oncoming blow, and holding the weapon firm in his grasp.

The masked foe strained and grunted as he tried to push or pull the club from Halsedric's hand. Soon after, Halsedric wrenched the weapon away from his opponent, leaving the abductor dumbstruck.

"Take him," snapped the man with the lamp, the urgency thick in his voice.

Without a weapon to bludgeon his prey, the masked foe reached into the folds of his clothes and produced a dagger. In the dark of that space and the dancing light, Halsedric and the hooded man struggled, fumbled, dodged, and grappled in the chaotic mix of light and shadow. Each thrust of the dagger was avoided, and each time Halsedric swung the club, the man withdrew.

In a blur of motion, their contest came to a swift and sudden end as the dark-clad attacker thrust when he should have dodged. With the man's own club, the warrior laid a savage blow to the head of his assailant. The club whooshed through the air before it connected, a sickening crunch sounding in the interior of that barn. At once, the masked foe fell lifeless to the ground with a hard thump.

A cry in the distance shattered the tension that crackled in the interior of the barn. Halsedric turned to the man with the lamp. In reply, the remaining abductor pulled a dagger from beneath the interior of his cloak. Halsedric spat on the ground, his pale eyes fixed on his would be captor with a cold and hostile stare.

Hounds barked in the distance. The noise they made distracted Halsedric for a moment. He stepped sideways and leaned to his left, diverting his gaze to the main house with a measure of concern. Just past the edge of the barn door opening, he could see the front entryway to the main house swing open. The pale orange light of a lamp poked out into the night. With it, the vague form of Farmer Hale appeared, standing in the middle of the doorway.

"Alarm, Alarm!" Farmer Hale cried out. "Bandits!"

Once more, Halsedric's attention shifted back to the third man with the lamp. Knowing misfortune followed those who came needlessly into his conflict, he knew he had to act quickly. He took one step forward. As he did, the foe with the lantern looked over both shoulders as he slowly backed away. The implication was clear as the man stuck out the dagger before him. If Halsedric took one more step forward, there would be consequences.

Fearing for the safety of the others, Halsedric decided to change tactics. Casting away the club, he turned about, stepped over to his sword, and plucked it from the ground. Rarely had he used the sword to take the lives of mortal men. Yet, it was a weapon far more intimidating than a club or a dagger, that was certain.

The move was poorly timed. As he came about, he noticed the lamp arcing through the air, flying into the barn. As if the world slowed, Halsedric watched the object rise and fall, finally hitting the hay-strewn dirt of the interior. When it landed, it crashed with a crack and a clang, oil spraying, spilling out, and catching fire. As many flames sprung up around the warrior, the owner of the lamp darted away, seeking to return from whence he came.

With a catastrophe brewing for his host, the warrior's concern shifted at once to the danger at hand. Halsedric began to stamp the ground with his feet, attempting to extinguish the tongues of blue, yellow, and red that grew and spread at an alarming rate. The leather soles of his boots thudded and scraped the dirt and hay—his efforts utterly in vain. With each attempt to quell the infant blaze, the flames only seemed to spread and grow. And with each inefficacious motion, the final abductor was closer to his escape.

"Roe!" shouted Halsedric. "Come!"

From the dark, Roe appeared, a blanket in hand. Casting the cloth on the fire and collapsing on top of it, the trapper cried out, "I got this!"

As Roe used the cloth to suffocate the flames, Halsedric turned, walking briskly to the barn entrance, before dashing around the side and into the fields.

His blood was up now. Ahead of Halsedric, many paces distant, was the dim form of the final attacker as he rushed headlong into the night. The warrior engaged, moving from a jog to a dash, as the third man sank further into the dark. Yet, the pursuit was short. After twenty or so strides, Halsedric slowed and broke off the chase. He might have been able to overtake the man if the cloak of night had not fallen. If he did continue his pursuit, it raised the question as to who or what might be waiting for him in the dark.

His safety was not his chief concern. Despite the momentary thrill of pursuit, reason and caution warned of the perils still behind him. There were three more being stalked by the huntress, and Farmer Hale had raised the alarm. Better still to attend to that than the questionable success of an uncertain capture.

Halsedric's feet sunk into the loose dirt of newly tilled fields as he slowed to a halt. A scowl gracing his youthful face, he stood there for a brief time and watched the featureless form of the third assailant melt into the evening's dark shroud. Despite the bitter taste it left in his mouth, letting a foe escape in that manner, he did not linger there long. Sword in hand, he turned away to join the fray of what might lie behind.

Justice, it seemed, would have to wait.

CHAPTER SIX

AFTER SLIDING THE BODY FROM THEIR CART, TWO sons of Farmer Hale grunted and strained as they carried their find—the remains of one of the attackers from the prior night. They shuffled with their burden across the ground, one son with his hands in the hollows of the dead man's arms, the other having a firm hold on the legs of the corpse. The dead man's cloak scraped the barren dirt as the head of the arrow that pierced his gut pointed to the sky. Streaked with blood, the head of the arrow danced as the body moved and swayed. Finally, as they positioned the corpse next to the others, they let go in unison. The body hit the ground with a sonorous thud, the shaft of Herodiani's arrow snapping in half beneath the dead weight of the corpse. A slight groan escaped the man's lips, garnering Halsedric's attention.

Flies had started to gather at the site, drawn by the scent of death from the dead man's three comrades. Not only had Halsedric slain two on his own accord, the huntress had taken two as well, or so it seemed. All four of the slain were clad head to toe in black, with black cloths over their faces to conceal their identities. Nameless, faceless men who came as specters, and departed as ghosts.

"Found him near the wood," said Arlen, one of Farmer Hale's sons as he pointed at the body he and his brother had just deposited. "Like a sack o' lead, he was," he added, swatting away a fly. The sons of Hale were taller and broader than their father, though they too had the same fine strands of black hair adorning their crowns. Like their father, their faces were round, though their chins were more pronounced than that of their sire.

The other son, Belgerid, left to tend to the horses hitched to the wagon. He spoke up as he returned to the horses. "Methinks there were more waitin' at the fringe of the trees. Hard to say, tho. Found a fresh mark of a hoof in the dirt. If'n they came by horse, no doubt one stayed behind to tend to 'em."

Three of Farmer Hale's hounds sniffed at the corpses as the familiar buzzing of insects continued to grow in intensity, winged creatures attracted by the ready spoil of dead flesh and dried blood. A perfect breeding ground for the next generation, even as the corpses started to bake in the rising heat of the day.

Wulf, one of Hale's younger progenies tapped the foot of the third body with the tip of his boot. "This one stopped twitchin' a while back. Ain't hearin' no breathin' either."

Halsedric took time to inspect the dead, walking up and down the line of corpses, laid out side-by-side in an orderly arrangement. The body, whom Wulf tapped with his boot, was the attacker whose head Halsedric pummeled with the club. Halsedric stepped around the bodies, standing across from Wulf, who stared at the warrior with wonder and expectation. Kneeling behind his victim's crown, he pushed the head to one side, then tilted it the other way, rigor not quite set in. Halsedric leaned forward and pulled back the hood that still shrouded the man's head, slipping his fingers beneath the black cloth of the mask. With a tug, he ripped the cloth effortlessly away from the dead man's face, the head lifting and falling back in response. Fully exposed now, one side of the man's face was bloated and bloody, the result of the beating Halsedric delivered. Further down, the pale eyes of the warrior spied a thin strap of leather just above the base of the neck. Wrapping his fingers around it, he tugged at it aggressively, causing the thong to snap. Ripping it free from the body, the warrior discovered the strap was attached to a disc of cast bronze, the diameter of it slightly smaller than the width of Halsedric's palm. Cradling the object in his hand as he felt its weight, Halsedric stood once more.

Wiping his brow with his sleeve, Arlen crouched down near the head of the man pierced through by the arrow. Reaching in and pulling the cloth from around the neck of the corpse, he revealed a jagged gash across the dead man's throat. "Slit `is throat, they did. Them's that stayed with the horses weren't takin' no chances he'd be livin' when they left `em behind." Blood covered much of the dead man's mouth and face, some of it dried.

He heard the words, but Halsedric offered no reply, preoccupied with his unexpected find. Wrapping the cord about his fingers, he lifted the medallion in the air, studying it for a time. Then he palmed it again, puzzling over the object. His thumb caressed the runes embossed on the disc. Runes of a familiar nature, though he had no insight into their meaning. Both sides of the medallion were inscribed thus, though the nature of the script on both sides differed. Transferring the disc to his left palm, he pulled his dagger from his belt. Using the pointed tip of the blade, he pierced his thumb, drawing blood. Returning the weapon to its sheath, he then pressed his pricked thumb against the disc of bronze, allowing the small stream of crimson fluid to flow out and into the valleys between the raised runes. At once, as the precious and holy fluid began to bubble and steam, Halsedric's brows lifted in surprise at the sight.

Holding the amulet by the strap, Halsedric looked now to the fourth body that lay on the ground. This man endured, perhaps, the worse fate of the four, and the work of Farmer Hale's hounds was clear for all to see. The dark cloth on the trousers and the cloak hinted at how aggressively the dogs fell upon him in their zeal to defend the farmer and his kin. Flies collected at the numerous wounds on his arms, the pale flesh pocked with pink tears where the teeth of the hounds tore at him. Rent cloth on the trousers also showed where one of the dogs went for his exposed legs, notably around his calf, the tough leather of his boots preventing some of the teeth from penetrating. Yet, the manner of his demise did not come by either the slashing teeth of the hounds or a well-aimed dart by the huntress, nor even by the swift thrust of her blade. From the man's neck stuck out the worn wooden handle of a knife, the blade of the weapon embedded deep into the dead man's flesh. Dark and bloody, the hand was soaked by the arterial spray of blood that shot out from the self-inflicted wound.

Herodiani knelt next to the dead man, a trinket of her own dangling from her fingers. Yet, when her free hand was not swatting away the flies, she stared at the embedded dagger with a sort of fascinated awe.

"Tell me again what happened to this man?" inquired Halsedric of the huntress.

"I have already spoken of this."

"Again, if you please."

She stood and stepped back, her hand continuing to bat away the flies that buzzed about her. The sound of the insects mingled with the clamor of nearby hens and the soft bleating of goats. "When I felled the first man, I relocated such that I might loose another dart." She motioned to the man whose arrow was stuck in his gut. "My first shot caused a great confusion. Fearing I might wound one of the beasts, I stayed my second shot when the hounds attacked. One hound fell upon the man who held the lamp, the other beast attacked the man you see before me. I slackened my bow and let it fall, drawing my sword instead.

The one who held the lamp pulled free from the jaws of the hound and ran, the beast in pursuit. The man I pierced with a dart also took to his feet and fled. He I pursued at first before returning, fearing I may stray too far from the main house. As I turned, I discovered the other hounds had joined its kin as they fell upon the prone mortal."

She paused for a moment, staring at the corpse. "He then—"

Her words turned whispery and uncertain, though she continued after a time. "He was prone, the hounds circling him as they attacked. He stabbed at them with his dagger, keeping them at bay. His eyes met mine even as I held my distance. Then, he turned his dagger upon himself."

"Twice?" inquired Halsedric.

"Twice, I believe. I did not take much notice past the first."

A quiet settled over the group for a time, the account leaving all those gathered there in shock. It was the huntress that broke the silence. Lifting the medallion by its leather band, she proclaimed, "He bore this about his neck."

A dark mark where blood had stained the leather of the band was clearly evident, and patches of dried blood collected in the grooves of the metal. A grim and mysterious trophy.

Arlen pulled a dagger from his belt and strode over to the second body laid out on the ground. He crouched, braving the ever-increasing swarm of insects as he cut away the cloth that covered the face of the deceased. Wisps of dark hair peeked out from the fringe of the hood as Wulf pulled it back to expose the face. Afterward, Arlen stood and returned the dagger to his belt before retreating from the flies.

Belgerid strode over and gazed down at the dead man's exposed face. His eyes narrowed as he studied the features of the fallen foe. "Lewland," he said after a time.

"Aye," Arlen said with a nod. "That be Lewland, alright."

"Lewland?" The name immediately caught Halsedric's attention.

"One of Fenian's kin," answered Arlen.

With a sharp, short whistle, Farmer Hale stepped around his sons, tapping the rear of one of the dogs. Both animals dutifully looked up to their master.

"Off with ye!" commanded Hale of the hounds, waving an arm in the air. It took another rebuke before the animals followed their master's command.

After the hounds trotted away, Hale gazed at the bodies, his hands set firmly on his hips. "Them Fenian! A bad brood they are. Naught but trouble, all of 'em." He spat on the ground, as if even mentioning the name of the clan left a sour taste in his mouth. "Ain't no surprise some o' 'em been in up to their necks with what's been goin' on 'round these parts."

Roe approached, standing next to Herodiani. He had been pacing around the gathering for some time, looking on from afar. Now he joined with the others. Gazing down at the man with the knife stuck in his neck, Roe's eyes narrowed as he took a half-pace forward and knelt. Getting a much closer look at the man, batting away the insects, he withdrew soon after.

Halsedric noticed Roe's sudden curiosity. "Do you know him?"

"Aye," Roe said as he lifted to his feet, clapping the soil from his hands. "I know him.

I've seen him in the village and down in Orem frequentin' the alehouses. He was there in the village when you came callin'."

"Do you have a name?" pressed Halsedric.

"Nah," Roe answered with a shake of his head. "But, I know he's one of Karne's men."

Noticing the medallion hanging from Herodiani's fingers, Roe stuck out his hand. "May I?"

Herodiani looked to Halsedric, questioning. After Halsedric nodded his approval, she offered the bronze token to the trapper.

Gingerly taking the medallion by the strap, Roe lifted the item to his eyes, inspecting the device as it pivoted and turned. Setting the object in his palm, he let the tips of his fingers caress the strange markings embossed in the coppery-hued metal.

"It is an evil thing," said Herodiani, her brilliant blue eyes watching Roe's interactions with the object. "Imbued with enchantments. To my touch, it burns like cold ice."

"I don't feel nothin'," answered Roe.

"Some magicks have no effect on Men, as they are fallen," answered Halsedric. "Agents of the Divine or those not of a fallen nature may be so affected." Holding up his prize, he gazed at the other medallion they confiscated. "These runes seem similar to those found in the tomb we visited in the year past." Unfolding the cloth, he ripped from the face of one of the fallen, Halsedric juggled the dangling medallion while laying the black cloth on his free palm. Carefully, he set the bronze token on top. Extending his open palm, Halsedric signaled Roe to lay the other there as well. It took Roe a moment before he understood what Halsedric was asking of him. After which, he left Herodiani's side, wandering around the bodies of the dead before placing the grim prize atop the other.

"Well, you're free to take all you find with you," Farmer Hale remarked. "We're believin' folk in these here lands. I ain't got no want for dark things in my house." He paused as he turned a jaded eye to the dead. "Trouble enough we got to bury this filth on good land." With a guttural, throaty noise, he churned up something foul and wet from his throat and spat on the dead.

After folding the remaining cloth around the bronze discs, Halsedric closed his fingers about the evil devices. He then knelt with one leg out, his forearms resting on his thigh. Head bowed, he offered a prayer to the Allfather, both reverent and silent. A quiet plea of mercy for those who were slain, and gratitude for the deliverance of his companions and his host. The others nodded their head in response, showing their respect for the act.

As Halsedric stood, Wulf lifted his head and stared at the warrior for a moment. "What'd you pray for? If'n I may ask."

"I offered gratitude for our deliverance," answered Halsedric. "And a prayer for the dead."

"For them?" Wulf pointed to the grisly scene at their feet, his face heavy with confusion and anger.

"Yes," answered Halsedric with a slow nod.

"After what they tried to do?"

"Yes," repeated Halsedric. Wulf himself seemed too confused for words, his eyes expressing more than his lips could say. A frustration and ire that someone would offer petitions for those who would have brought misfortune to them all.

"Show some respect, boy," chided Hale.

Halsedric lifted his hand to the patriarch of the clan and bid peace between the two. In the ensuing silence, he turned to Wulf and addressed him. "Many evil men I have encountered over my many years. And without exception, each fell into evil for one of three reasons. Some embraced it willingly, seeking to sate some hunger they had within. Power. Lust. Avarice. Renown. Then there are those who sought evil to justify some imagined wrong. Those who succumb to the seduction of pride are chief among these."

He looked down for a moment at the battered face of the man he slew with a club. "Then there are those who hold true griefs and hardships. Who wait patiently for justice that never arrives. In their anger and grief, they seek a darker path for the reckoning they are owed. And in doing so, lose themselves.

Even among the most selfish, there is still salvation for those who desire it. Yet, in death, all hope for reclamation is lost, and only final judgment awaits."

Halsedric's hand waved slowly across the line of corpses. "Do you know what truly lies in the hearts and minds of these men? Have you lived their lives? Seen and felt their misfortunes?" He then looked up to Wulf with expectant eyes.

Wulf stared dumbly back. The anger the young man once displayed fled from his face like water washing away soil. Yet, all he did was stare, offering no reply to Halsedric's inquiry.

"Do not, then, judge too harshly even those who desire evil upon you. For we all are fallen, resistant to the Will of the Allfather, and deserve death. We still may find salvation and redemption so long as there is breath within us. They shall not."

Halsedric turned to Farmer Hale. "There may be reprisals. We will call for aid to protect you and your kin."

Farmer Hale let out a brief but defiant chuckle. "Let 'em come." Pointing to the man at Herodiani's feet, he answered, "That one didn't fare so well. And I'll send the boys out to warn the folk hereabouts what's gone on. For all their bold talk, them Fenian ain't much for a standup fight." He looked up at Halsedric, flinty faced and one eye pinched. With steel in his words, he added, "Ain't no harder folk than them tendin' these lands. If'n they wanna come...let 'em come."

Partly amused and heartened by the farmer's bold words, Halsedric let a small grin slip. "Very well then."

Like a general in a desperate pitched battle, Hale went about commanding his sons to action, apportioning some for burial detail, while sending Wulf to tend to the morning chores on their farm. As he did, Roe turned to face Halsedric again and said, "I was plannin' on takin' you two to the Gallain 'stead. Mayhaps we should head out—"

"Karne, you said?" Halsedric pivoted quickly, interrupting the trapper.

"Karne?" It took Roe a moment to remember the association of the name to that of one of the dead men. "Aye," he answered with a nod.

"He lives in the city?"

"Aye," answered Roe, a confused look on his face.

"We have some time," continued Halsedric. "Take us to the city of Orem. I want to inquire further into this man and his associations."

At once, a muted look of fear graced Roe's expression. His hand reached out and gently touched Halsedric's arm, as if subconsciously trying to stay the warrior. "Karne is a Lord of Orem. He ain't no one to be triflin' with. Better we head out to the Gallain 'stead."

"Let me shoulder that concern," replied Halsedric as he set about tucking the wrapped medallions into a pocket on his vest. "Make ready our departure. I want to be away, and soon."

He then joined Herodiani, drawing close. The huntress gazed up at him as Halsedric bent down slightly, her bright blue eyes contrasted against his pale irises. In a whisper, he said, "We have need of aid from our friends."

"How many?" said the huntress in kind.

"Six, I think."

"Have them encamp here?" asked Herodiani.

To this question, Halsedric paused, his eyes shifting away for a moment. "No. I do not think there will be much need for that. Have them maintain a watch from a goodly distance. I do not suspect the compatriots of our deceased friends desire more of what they received. Still, better to err on the side of caution." He paused, then asked. "Do you think the hounds will create trouble?"

Herodiani answered with a grin. "No. They may be fierce in the face of mortals. But to my kin, they will bare more belly than tooth."

CHAPTER SEVEN

HALSEDRIC LIFTED THE MEDALLION BY ITS leather strap as he leaned in closer to the fire. The campfire snapped and hissed as if it, too, hated the very presence of the thing. The wind gusted slightly, sending smoke swirling, stinging the warrior's eyes. He did little to acknowledge the annoyance he felt. His attention was on those raised markings and the secrets they contained.

The trio spent a greater portion of the day in travel, halting to make camp before the sun vanished behind the western horizon. Roe guided them west to the river, the waters leading them south where the river fed into the lake. Here, upon the shores of the lake of the same name, the city of Orem was located. Roe preferred to use the waterways as guides to his travels for obvious reasons. It was easier to water the horses and easier to locate food, if so needed. Those who lived in the western regions of the Orem were also less troublesome.

Whatever goods Roe acquired at the village, he left with Farmer Hale along with one of his horses. They were riding light and fast, taking only what provisions they required for the trek. It was a four-day ride before they'd reach the outskirts of Orem; three if they pushed themselves.

Now encamped, the rumble of the wind, and the popping and snapping of the fire was matched by the low hiss of rushing water over stones. When the salty smoke wasn't invading his nostrils, Halsedric could smell the gentle scent of the nearby water in the air. From the shallows, frogs croaked and chirped a subtle and rhythmic song in the night that offered a strange sense of peace in a land where a threat seemed to brew, despite several years of quiet.

"What do the markings mean?" asked Roe, laid out on top of a blanket, head propped up on his hand.

Halsedric's eyes never lifted from the medallion. "As of yet, I do not know. As I wintered in Elenur, I spent much time in the library of Lord Aurogeloi, seeking answers to the mystery of these markings."

"A strange name, that."

The medallion lowered from Halsedric's gaze, and his eyes fixed on that of Roe. "Aurogeloi?"

"Aye."

"Indeed," answered Halsedric, his eyes downturned for a moment. "A true mouthful at times, or so my mother would proclaim. He is the foster-father of Herodiani, and a gracious host. He has an extensive collection of books and scrolls from ages that extend far past the knowledge of men and their reckonings."

"And what did you find?"

Halsedric sighed and his head tipped down slightly. "Very little." He paused for a second, and with a hint of frustration in his voice, added, "I wish I had taken the time to scribe the markings I found. Alas, I did not have such foresight to take quill and ink with me on my journey. An oversight I regret. One that I will not repeat."

Roe looked about. "Is the maid on guard again?"

"Yes," Halsedric answered in a near-automatic tone.

"Is that all she's good for?"

Halsedric paused for a moment, his eyes lifting from the medallion before fixing on Roe. "She offers much in the manner of aid in the tasks I am given. Does her presence trouble you?"

"No," Roe answered softly, head bowed. "Just ponderin'." He paused for a moment, then continued. “Just that I’ve heard about you…what the tales tell and all. I didn’t figure you’d be needin’ someone to be watchin’ over you and all.”

The leather strap that held the medallion wound like a tiny snake in Halsedric’s palm as he returned the bronze disc to the cloth that contained it. “What is it that you think I do, friend?”

Roe looked up and shrugged. “Slay monsters and evil men, from what they say.”

Halsedric shot Roe a quick, steely glance. “I stare into the Abyss. I hunt shadows and ghosts. Devils and demons. Yerch. Morgur. Attin. The things that normal men speak of only in whispers and rumors. Thus, it is that the Allfather has bestowed upon me those gifts to further such ends.”

“Explainin’ why that one tough looked like his face had been caved by a maul?” said Roe.

Covered now in the dark cloth of the dead man’s mask, Halsedric set his grim trophies aside. “Strength of limb, yes.”

“Strength?” Roe sniffed a laugh. “You shattered the man’s skull! And you moved like lightnin’."

“Indeed,” Halsedric interrupted. “Necessities of the trade. Yet, despite the many gifts bestowed upon me by the Allfather, the heart of a mortal man still beats in my breast. I have but two hands. I still have need of sleep. I need aid in binding and unbinding wounds. And,

I oft have need of a guide, hence your participation in this endeavor.

I swim in waters both perilous and unforgiving. Having those around me whom I can trust is, I believe, a wise course of action."

He looked down at the medallions as he covered them over with the fringes of the tattered cloth, pausing for a moment. His face shadowed concern in the orange dancing glow of the campfire, his silence as thick and brittle as ice.

"But?" asked Roe, expectantly.

Halsedric continued his silence for a moment after, his expression unable to hide the trouble that plagued his heart. As he stuffed the wrapped parcel of tokens into a pouch on his belt, Halsedric spoke slowly but purposefully. "The pursuit of peril is ever a gamble. Many years I have known Herodiani. She is my friend. Ever do I warn her of the consequence of casting lots. Yet, for all her skill and wisdom, she can be headstrong. She persists in her devotion to my cause. I am called to my tasks. She is not."

"Were you born for this life?"

"No," answered Halsedric with a shake of his head. "I was not as you know me now. I was a soldier long ago. Slain before the last battle of a terrible war. It was the Prophet Jalamil who found me. By the hand of the Allfather, my flesh was reclaimed and a new mantle bestowed upon me."

"Wait!" Alarmed, Roe lifted up slightly. "You knew Jalamil?"

"Yes," answered Halsedric with a slight nod.

"You lived in the time of Jalamil?"

"I think that requires no further explanation. Yes."

For a moment, Roe looked at Halsedric dumbfounded. When he spoke, his words were whispery and laced with fascination. "That means, you're…you're—"

"Very old, yes," Halsedric answered.

"But you look—"

"Indeed. I do not age, so long as the mantle of the Allfather is still upon me. For this reason, I winter with the Elanni, for they do not feel the touch of time as well." With a sudden change in expression, Halsedric inquired, "Enough of me. Tell me your story."

"Ain't nothin' much to tell."

"Many a woodsman I have dealt with in my time," Halsedric countered. "You seem to know the wilds well, yet your tongue has a western flavor to it. And you seem to know too much about the ways of city life. Servants and estates. Alehouses and where nobles gather. Of the many huntsmen I have known, few of them know the ways of such a life, and even fewer are willing to venture to such places. Rather they would trade in the villages than to dare the dangers of the cities."

"Aye, true," answered Roe. "I was once a city dweller in my youth. Your sense is keen." He paused for a moment before continuing. "I was born and raised in the city of Messel, along the River Adonne. You heard of it?"

"Yes," said Halsedric, his head bobbing. "One who has known naught save the city now a seasoned trapper? It must be a curious tale."

"That it is," Roe said, his head nodding slowly. His hand shifted a bit underneath the weight of his head.

"Well, I weren't no nobleman's son, that be for sure. Never knew my father. And my mother? Well, I won't mention what she did for her silver. 'Twas a strange and terrible thing, a young'un to be raised in such places."

Roe's eyes set in a thoughtful faraway stare. "You've got to be tough to live on the streets, and quick. That was me, filching a purse or two for coin. I was good at it, too. As quick as a whip, I was. Wild like a rabbit in the fields. I found a home wherever it was dry, and I found it a special treat in duckin' the city guard.

Then one day, I came across this old man with a big old loaf in his hands." Roe lifted his hands and splayed his fingers to approximate an object roughly the size of a man's forearm. "Well, that was enough for me. I snatched it away, running off somewhere with my prize. Mighty proud of myself, I was. A fine meal from an easy mark. I still remember how full I was afterwards.

The next day, I saw the old man again at the same place near the market. He was just sittin' there on a stone step, another loaf in his hands. As if he were waiting for someone. Well, my eye saw that fat loaf. As quick as you can wink, I snatched it away and was off as quick as a rabbit bein' chased by a fox."

A sigh and a laugh escaped Roe's lips before he continued his tale. "Mighty proud, I was, havin' another fine meal that night. I never stopped to think about the old man or who he was waitin' for. My belly was full. That was enough for me."

Like an actor feigning surprise, Roe continued his tale. "So then, another day, and two easy marks in a row, I go to the same spot by the market. There he is! The old man. Another loaf. I can't believe my luck. So, I swipes another easy meal. And the next day, there he is again. And another loaf. And the next day. And the next. And another..."

Roe's voice trailed off as he sat up in full, crossing his legs on the ground. The trapper went strangely silent for a time, the actions of a man meditating on something profound and sad. Clearing his throat, his voice softer now, Roe went on. "That old man was the prophet Wolland. For two years, I reckon, I followed him where he traveled," Roe continued. "I learned the worship of the Allfather, the ways of salvation, and the hope that His words brought." He then let slip a shallow smile as he unconsciously grabbed at his ear. "We traveled to the highlands, south of the Village of Bright, and stayed with a huntsman there. Gussman was his name. Strong in the Faith and an old friend of Wolland. *Grumblin' Gussman*, the locals called him. A tough ol' cuss, but not to the prophet. Treated him like a long-lost brother. Greeted him with open arms."

Breathing deep the air and letting it flow slowly out of his nose, Roe changed his demeanor. Reverence tinged with sadness gave way to a strange sort of awe, made plain by wide eyes and the tone of his voice. "It was durin' that time that I grew to love open spaces. The clean air. The quiet, and the mystery of the wilds. The sound of rain on the leaves and the silence of the forest. Lookin' up at the sky at night without the lamplight in the way. Seein' the endless mystery of the stars and the moon.

Ol' Wolland must have seen this in me when he asked Gussman if'n I might be trained in the ways of the wilds. To hunt and fish and trap. Gussman never denied nothin' to the prophet, so he took me in. For many years after, I lived with the old fox, learnin' everything he could teach and more. You might say I was called to this life, if'n that's what it be—a callin'.

Only when the old fox fell ill did I see Wolland again. As if he knew it was his friend's time. That was when the prophet spoke of his need for people like me. The mission I now got."

Roe paused and his head fell in contemplation. "How could I refuse the man whose kindness took me away from the wretched life I led? So, here now I am. With you."

"You ever miss the life of the cities?" asked Halsedric.

"Not a wit," answered Roe with a sniff.

Head up now, Roe returned Halsedric's gaze. "An' if'n I might be so bold—you don't sound like no soldier. I've known a few in my time as well."

By now, Halsedric had picked up his sword and laid it in his lap, his fingers on the scabbard. Looking past his brows, he replied. "I was born the son of a wealthy merchant."

"Aye," Roe said with a slow nod. "I could tell by the speech and the manner."

"Manner?"

"Them wealthy types have an air about them. Don't take much to figure it out."

"Air?" said Halsedric, slightly confused. He knew his speech was refined and easily stuck out in the company of those considered "common." Having clearly identifiable mannerisms, however, was a new revelation.

"Aye," answered Roe coldly. "Like a man of privilege. One tended to by servant folk and such."

"True," replied Halsedric with a nod. "I was well educated. The house of my father had many who attended it."

Lifting his head and plucking a thin stick from the ground, Halsedric twirled the limb in his fingers as he continued his own recounting. "When I was but sixteen years of age, the War of the Prophets raged. Martial orders of the Faithful were raised to train warriors to fight for the cause."

"Never heard of it," Roe interjected.

"It was a long time past," said Halsedric.

After a moment's pause, Halsedric continued his story. "I and my brother were offered to the cause by my father. For several years I trained and fought until one day—the last known battle of that war—I was slain. I and my comrades were moving in secret to attack the enemy who had marshaled their strength upon a hilltop. It was hoped that we might fall upon the enemy, unawares. Yet, we were betrayed."

"By whom?"

"One of our own," replied Halsedric, tamping the end of the twig into the hard ground. "A friend of mine, I confess. Seduced by the Prophetess and swayed to her cause."

Halsedric paused for a moment, his busy fingers now still for several seconds. "The last thing I remember were the howls of painted men, the screams of the dying, and a bloody axe that fell before all went dark."

"The Prophet Jalamil came that I might be raised again. He consecrated my dead flesh to the will of the Allfather, God of the West. And so, I became as you know me now."

"Chosen," said Roe softly.

"Many are called. Few are chosen."

"And where'd you hear that?"

"Jalamil," replied Halsedric.

Through narrowed lids, Roe hummed his answer, all of it signaling a subtle disbelief. "I'm not a man of learnin' and such, but I've heard such words before. Nobles and the like settin' themselves above common folk with such high-minded talk. It ain't what Wolland taught me." He thought for a moment, then asked, "What was Jalamil like?"

"He was a tall man. Dark. Clothed in a threadbare robe," answered Halsedric. "His shoes were well worn, if he wore them at all. He oft ate porridge mixed with wild nuts that he foraged, and honey when nature favored him. He lived such a life until he found his end at a Hakanese spear."

Halsedric's head dipped, and he was silent for a time, pondering what he might say next. His head raised quickly as he spoke. "To be called—to be chosen. Such titles are spoken wistfully by those who know them not. Jalamil was chosen, even before birth, yet his clothing was poor, his daily portion simple. To be chosen is not a crown worn in glory. It is a yoke. To be chosen is not to be served, but to serve until your days end. A burden shouldered by those whose reward comes not in this life, but the next.

There are some who envy my long years," Halsedric continued. "Yet, my days are not my own, nor is my purpose in this world." His hand lazily pointed at Roe. "You may wander where the spirit takes you. You can enter into marriage and sire a family if it so pleases you. I cannot. I go where I am bidden and do as I must."

Roe started to speak, but Halsedric was not done. "I have seen glories whereupon you would cast yourself to the ground, trembling, and hide your face in fear. And I have gazed into the Abyss from whence evil comes unto the world, witnessing sights that would drive men to madness. Sights that would haunt your dreams until the ending of your days.

Thus, I was made, and to such ends I go, to dispatch the Will of the Allfather. He who has raised me and set me on my course. My life a mere consequence of the ends by which the Allfather seeks to lift Man from darkness into everlasting light and life."

A dread quiet fell between the pair, Roe stewing in a stunned sort of silence. When he was able to summon the words, they were softer. "I, too, have seen a darker side of life, especially in the streets. What men say. What they do. How they twist what is true and right, leavin' those such as me in the dirt."

"Not all men are thus."

Roe thought on this for a time, then asked, "You cannot take for yourself a woman?"

"To what end?" replied Halsedric. "To watch them grow old and perish? To see my sons rise up and perish as well?"

"So, forever you shall be lonely and alone?"

Halsedric thought on this for a time, casting the twig he held into the fire. "Perhaps, one day, the life I lost shall be returned to me. That I might once more have restored that which was taken from me by that wildman's axe. Till such day arrives, there is naught but the mission and its conclusion."

The conversation fell into a lull, Halsedric gazing down at his blade, his fingers reaching out, running the length of his scabbard. Roe gazed at the fire contemplatively. After a time, the trapper spoke. "What became of that Prophetess you spoke of?"

"She is dead," answered Halsedric coldly.

"What?" Roe's attention quickly turned to that of the holy warrior.

"She is dead," repeated Halsedric.

"How'd you know?"

"Because it was I who slew her."

Roe stared at Halsedric for a time, a slow flush of red overtaking his cheeks. When he did speak, it was low and filled with confusion. "A woman?"

Halsedric looked up, dispassionately. "Yes."

A palpable tension filled the air between the two. Roe's face twisted with perplexity and anger as he asked his question again. "You slew...a woman?"

"Yes," Halsedric answered again, this time confusion in his tone.

"If'n that don't say it all," Roe exclaimed angrily. "Such a man that drags a fair maid with him into danger and all." He paused for a moment, heated eyes seeming to bore a hole right through the holy warrior. "What man puts a woman to the sword?"

"It was my mission," answered Halsedric quickly. Even as Roe started to speak, Halsedric swiftly interrupted. "You were not there. It was before your time. You did not see what I and others had seen. The bodies hanging from the trees. The altars stained with the blood of the faithful and those who resisted her foul demands. Do not speak in rash condemnation of things you know little. I was there. I did as I was commanded to do."

Roe was silent for a time, his cheeks still burning and wroth. When he did speak, his wavering voice hinted at the anger he restrained with each syllable he spoke. "You remember the word you spoke to me on the hill beneath the willows?"

It took Halsedric a moment to recall the password he had said days past. "Vellamilla. Yes. I remember."

"Did they tell you the meanin' behind the name?"

Halsedric shook his head in response.

"'Twas the name of my mother. The woman who birthed me. Do you know how she came to her end?"

Halsedric answered softly, his eyes closing slowly. "No." He suspected just where this conversation was going.

"Slain by a man. To avoid payin' gold for her favors." Silence followed, Roe's hatred building, each word he spoke like the stabbing point of a knife. "She weren't much of a mother, but she was mine. And now she's dead. Forever lost to me."

"And for that, you have my sympathy."

"Tell me, friend," Roe spat back, "why then should I follow one who openly takes it upon themselves to slay a woman? Like my mother?"

"You were not there, and you do not understand—"

"Oh, I understand well enough," Roe answered sharply, his head shaking and his brows lifted high.

The pair stared at each other in silence, their faces painted by the weaving flames of the campfire. It was Halsedric who shattered the tense and fragile quiet.

"I tire," said Halsedric as he lifted his sword and set it aside. "Enough has been spoken this night. Rest is needed for the long journey tomorrow. Perhaps silence will allow cooler heads to prevail."

More silence followed as Halsedric stretched himself out on the ground, laying his head on his pack. All the while, Roe watched him with an unrelenting stare. It took a time before the warrior was able to find sleep. It came all the same.

The next day of travel was as quiet as it was tense. The trek was uneventful in itself, Roe leading them south using the waters of the Upper Orem as his guide. Halsedric and Herodiani spoke openly with one another as circumstances dictated. Roe, however, was curiously morose and silent. When he did speak to the others, it was only at need. And when he addressed Halsedric, the angry glare in the trapper's eyes was impossible to ignore.

That night, when they made camp, Halsedric considered trying to address what he knew bothered Roe—the fact that he had slain a woman. A sin that, in the eyes of the trapper, was an unforgivable, damnable offense. After making a fire of wood and dung, the trio ate their nightly meal in near silence before Herodiani left the others to keep watch. Halsedric made his nightly petitions and prayers, seeking wisdom in healing the rift that now divided the group. When he was done, he sat about the smoky campfire as the trapper puffed on his pipe, doing his best to ignore the presence of the holy warrior. In the long and sullen silence that lingered as the pair sat across from one another, a beggarly fire between them, he pondered the wisdom of raising the subject once more. In the end, Halsedric decided to leave things as they were, in the hope that time and the better nature of the trapper might heal this sudden division.

"Rest well," Halsedric said with a half-hearted smile as he took to his bed—one blanket on the ground, and his cloak over top. The most he received from Roe was a grunt.

What rest the warrior found was brief. Halsedric was nudged awake. The fire was near its ebb, red glowing coals being the only light that availed him. When his eyes opened, he saw a shadowy figure kneeling next to him.

"The trapper is gone." Herodiani's words were whispery and sounded urgent. "Should we pursue?"

It took Halsedric a moment to let the pronouncement set in. He sat up, and through bleary eyes scanned the darkened camp around him. For a long time, he wondered in silence, his face pained. A breeze blew, and something cried out in the night, the sharp shrill screech of some small rodent. In time, the warrior answered. "Let him go."

"We still need a guide."

Once more, head down, he withdrew into thought. When he spoke, he did so after a sigh. "We have the river as our guide. That will have to do. We must trust to faith that the Allfather will provide."

Pulling his blanket back around him, Halsedric lay back down, turning onto his side. "We will discuss this further, come dawn."

CHAPTER EIGHT

THE TRIP TO OREM WASN'T PARTICULARLY arduous or eventful, save for a few of the residents whose parcels extended to the banks of the river. Most established their households on higher ground, leaving the rich soil of the floodplain for their crops. Yet, this was not always the case. On one occasion, Halsedric was accused of trespassing by a farmer and his sons. They were initially bold in their confrontation, bringing clubs and pitchforks to the encounter. The warrior's fearless demeanor, not to mention the blade he carried, was enough for the homesteaders to keep their distance. Still, the pair continued on until near nightfall, finding a spot where they could encamp for the night, unmolested.

On the last day of their trek, they came upon a tower atop a bald hill. Finding shelter behind a high outcrop of brown stone, the two travelers reconnoitered the structure from afar, seeking movement or signs of life. The tower itself looked weatherworn and poorly maintained, an exterior walkway just below the roof having collapsed at points along its run. The high pickets that surrounded the base of the fortification had either toppled over or rotted away.

It was mutually agreed that a closer inspection of the tower was a prudent course of action. Herodiani led the way, leaving her bow behind, relying on her sword instead. Pulling up the hood of her cloak and blending into the terrain, she went forth to scout the structure.

Halsedric waited patiently with the horses, their mounts either lying in the grass near the rock or using the stone outcrop as cover. These lands were wild and untouched by pick or plow, the nearest homestead nearly a league distant. From where he crouched, he could see the rippling waters of the lake through the trees. This was prime land, and he wondered why it was left to remain wild. Most of the land they crossed had long tilled rows and flocks of sheep grazing on the abundant grasses. He could only conclude that it was reserved by the lords of the city itself, perhaps as a forward outpost whose use was no longer required. A place to observe the comings and goings of bandits and raiders in order to sound an alarm and muster the city guard. Still, in other places, shepherds were never forbidden to range their flocks even in reserved lands, especially where water was easily obtained.

A warbling whistle sounded—a faraway signal from Herodiani indicating all was clear. At once, the resting horses rose, Halsedric mounting one as it did. The gathering then ascended the slope of the hill to the base of the tower.

The tower itself was three stories high, whose walls were made of cut stone and mortar. The base was windowless, save for several slits from which archers could loose their arrows. On the second story, a singular window was set in the center of each face where watchmen could survey the land from the four cardinal directions. While it may have been occupied at one time as a garrison, it was clearly no longer inhabited. Rotted and fallen slats from its peaked roof littered the ground, the mortared joints between the irregular cut stone having fractured and crumbled. Other buildings once stood in the space surrounded by the pickets, but these had suffered the same fate.

Hood back, Herodiani stood by the doorway to the interior of the tower. With a swift motion, she returned her sword to its scabbard, whistling a second time and lifting her hand in the air. Soon after, a fluttering sound was heard as a bird swooped in, its wings splayed and flapping. Its feet forward and digits outstretched, the creature landed gracefully on her hand. Slightly larger than a cardinal or a lark, the plumage of the bird was as blue as a clear summer sky, save for the crest which was the hue of fiery embers. As its head turned and tilted, the bird let out two sharp chirps, one gleaming black eye seemingly fixed on that of the huntress.

Herodiani transferred the bird to her right shoulder as the horses approached, Halsedric dismounting not far from where the Elanni huntress stood. The warrior's boots hit the ground with a deep thud as he dismounted.

Thick posts and a beam formed the doorway of the structure, carved from a light gray stone, perhaps granite. A hard dense door of oak swung upon hinges made of black iron, the planks that formed the barrier reinforced by iron braces. While the metal resisted the encroach of time and the elements, it was still ill-kept and rusting.

"Naught have visited here for some time," said Herodiani at her companion's approach. "What few tracks I have found are very old. Weeks, perhaps. It is difficult to tell."

Halsedric pushed back the door before staring at the interior. Inside the tower was musty, water having infiltrated somewhere above despite the dirt floor being as dry as old bones.

Dead weeds and creepers had invaded the interior through the arrowslits, and more than a few dead leaves had been swept in by the wind. Light streamed in from the space in what openings the vegetation had not clogged. Shadows clung to the corners and niches, and stray feathers littered the floor, left behind by the former occupants who had fled when the huntress entered the interior. Above them, round lengths of smaller trees were used as rafters upon which the floorboards of the upper level were affixed. Shelves made from cut stone stuck out from the wall, stained yellow and white, an unpleasant reminder of the feathered creatures that now called the tower home. Upon a stony perch, now evacuated, the bird of blue and orange found a suitable spot to reside.

A crude ladder ascended to the second level. Herodiani scaled the rungs with a deft and cautious motion. While the huntress moved swift and silent, it was Halsedric's investigations that made the most racket. Dried vines and dead grasses crunched beneath his feet. His blade scraped on the stone as it probed and pushed back piles of debris. In time, his eye caught a glimpse of something white just beneath a pile of dead vegetation and moss in a corner near the door. Gently using the tip of his sword, he cleared away a pile that covered the lower portion of the eastern wall. His efforts exposed lettering painted on the irregular stone.

Sheathing his blade and kneeling at the spot, he pulled away what remained.

The paint was not fresh, flecks of it having chipped away long ago. These were runes, whose design was familiar to his eyes—three of them in a line. At once he stood and reached into a pouch on his belt, seeking the wrapped medallions they took from the dead men at the Hale farm. Kneeling once more and pulling back the cloth that covered the tokens, Halsedric went about comparing the raised writing in the bronze to what was painted on the wall.

While similarities existed, the markings themselves were different. Still, these were foreign to any written script he could remember, and eerily like the writing he discovered on the wall of the tomb in the Aranach.

Halsedric stood up and scanned the bronze discs, lost in thought, pondering the meaning of what he uncovered. Eventually, Herodiani drew close to him, her stare directed at Halsedric's discovery.

"More of those foul runes, I see," she muttered.

Halsedric looked over at his companion. "What did you discover?"

"There is naught above," Herodiani said with a shake of her head. "The ladders and the timbers of the floor above will bear your weight, should there be a need to ascend. The uppermost floor is unsuitable for you, I fear.

Rot has crept into the wood. There, I may go. You would be ill-advised to do so."

"And what of the lands near the city? Is there a proper place that we might make camp?"

"I have spied a hill further south where we could encamp." Herodiani's eyes lifted and her head tilted to one side. "Though, this would be a fine spot. From here, it is less than half a league to the fringe of the city—a brief ride from where we stand. The land here is lonely enough from what I have seen."

Halsedric turned away and departed the interior of the tower, stepping out into the green grass of the hilltop. He set about wrapping the bronze tokens with the cloth that contained them. "This very well may be a meeting place for the same villains who came for us some nights ago."

"If this is true, none have gathered here in many days," countered Herodiani. "We are far enough from the city that our presence here might go unnoticed." She turned and surveyed the landscape about them. "None seem to occupy this place. I do not understand—"

"Perhaps there are rumors of the tower, keeping others at bay," interrupted Halsedric as he returned the medallions to a pouch on his belt. "Perhaps there is greater danger here than either of us know."

"How then would another hill suffice, if it may be seen from this height?" countered Herodiani. "Better *we* hold the higher ground."

"To hold the high ground is to also defend it."

Herodiani looked around at the Lenogala mounts that accompanied them on their journey. "I will not be alone in doing so." As she spoke the words, two of the horses nodded their heads and snorted.

His face strained, Halsedric inhaled deep, exhaling a long and noisy sigh. He paused for a moment, his gaze settling on the southern horizon.

"Very well," he mumbled. "I think this ill-advised. Yet, if you are assured this spot is suitable, I will not argue."

Herodiani approached and stood next to Halsedric, gently placing her hand on the hilt of her sword. "Now that we are here, how then do you intend to find this Karne?"

"I have a notion or two."

Her head turning and looking up at Halsedric, Herodiani gazed at him quizzically. "How then?"

He was slow to answer. "When a wealthy man of questionable means ascends to sudden prominence, what is often the means by which it is obtained?"

The eyes of the huntress shifted momentarily as she pondered the question. "Tar?"

"Tar," parroted Halsedric in a low and rumbling tone.

CHAPTER NINE

DAYS HAD PASSED SINCE HERODIANI LAST SAW Halsedric. Her last glimpse of him was as he passed beneath the canopy of a small wood. A cluster of trees whose boundaries ended at a cluster of dwellings thrown together along the main road that led to the city gates. A place of chaotic and despairing masses of hastily erected shelters whose fires and ovens cast up a hazy smog. A cloud so thick and pernicious that made it impossible to discern anyone among the mass of denizens of Orem from the other, even with her keen Elanni eyes. While her confidence in her friend's abilities was unchallenged, there was always that twinge of doubt that passed through her thoughts like a needle piercing skin. Peril was a constant in their journeys, their only safe harbor being the blessed realms of her kindred. Only there was peace assured, in a world still marred by war and the unending certainty of men.

So, it was she who maintained her thankless vigil in that rotting tower, alone in the second story, their things piled in one corner of the room where she sat and watched the world, both north and south. Counting the hours with the faint sound of a bell that rang in the city some distance away. The only break in the monotony of her routine was the occasional meal and venturing out into the countryside to check on the Lenogala who sheltered and fed on a nearby patch of land.

Such were the details of her part in Halsedric's mission. A path she chose willingly, and with few regrets. Long hours and days of tedium and boredom, punctuated by moments of terror and travail. Facing darkness that few, even among her kin, would dare to face. Confronting horrors that would freeze the blood of mortals.

Now, it was one such night when an unexpected visitor approached. Arriving from the north, the figure wore dark clothing. In their possession, they held a lamp whose flame was a wax candle sheltered by panes of glass set into a frame of brass. There was a moment of euphoria as she tracked the figure moving beneath the trees, thinking that it might be Halsedric returning to relieve her from her thankless watch. Yet, as the figure stepped out onto open land, such hopes were dashed. He was too tall, too round, his pace too noisy, and his steps too uneven. Even as he ascended the hill on which the tower was located, she could hear the labored breaths as the man struggled to reach the top. As he crested the hill and neared the crumbling structure, he raised his lamp and lifted his head, giving her a brief glimpse of what hid beneath the folds of his hood, a long face with puffed cheeks whose nose and mouth were covered by a mask of black cloth.

Withdrawing from the window, she avoided the man's gaze, for it was a man by all the signs she saw. With her cloak hiding her from his eyes, she slowly drew her dagger with utmost care to not make a sound. Her heart raced as she anticipated trouble.

If trouble was to come, it was clear to her that she had better than even odds of victory. Beneath where she sheltered, she could hear the man standing near the doorway, breathing heavily, no doubt leaning against the exterior stone wall as he caught his breath. He may have had a good ten stones of weight to counter her thin and seemingly fragile frame. Yet, the fortitude he displayed was lacking, to say the least. One thrust or slash from her sword, and he would be done for.

The pale light that leaked up from the narrow gaps in the floorboards grew in intensity as she rose and silently withdrew to the southeastern corner, just opposite the hole where the ladder poked up from the floor below. She eyed the pile of their things that lay in a heap diagonally across from where she crouched, knowing full well that if that shambling heap decided to search the tower, it would not be long before she would be discovered. Setting aside her dagger, she pulled back her cloak and laid her hands upon the hilt of her sword. Using the noise the stranger made below as a cloak of another kind, she drew her main weapon in preparation for a fight. A fight that seemingly would never come. Even as the stranger recovered his stamina over the course of many minutes, he did not ascend the ladder. His obnoxious huffs and puffs were reduced to the occasional noisy exhale and groans of final relief. The light below never moved from where it had set, Herodiani half-tempted to find a suitable gap in the boards and peer below. What followed was a long siege of sorts as Herodiani waited for the man to ascend in the tense quiet. Twice the bells in the city rang in the distance. Two hours passed as the siege continued. With each moment that passed after the first bell rang, the likeliness of a confrontation dwindled as the night dragged on.

From time to time, the man below shuffled about, stepping outside the tower, no doubt checking the position of the moon. This she used as an opportunity to reposition herself to one of the four openings in the wall. She checked the landscape, looking for movement, wondering if others were coming.

"Late, as usual," the stranger grumbled under his breath in a voice that was low, rough. Words flavored with the same mode and manner of speech she heard spoken at the Hale homestead.

No longer troubled with the concern of being discovered any time soon, she went about keeping watch at each window, repositioning after a time, taking pains to make no noise as she moved. She was about to relocate from her southern watch to that of the west when her keen Elanni eyes detected movement. There she remained, staring at the same forest fringe where Halsedric vanished from her view, her patience rewarded in time.

Two men soon appeared in a nearby clearing, one of them leading the way with a lamp. Both men were clad in dark clothes, cloaked and hooded. She shifted slightly as she watched them approach and ascend the hill, pausing at the base of the tower and vanishing from her view. There, in the stillness beneath the cloudless sky, she heard the scraping of steel against brass, reminiscent of daggers being drawn. The light that shone up in the gaps of the floorboards grew as the light of one lamp joined with that of the other.

"Brief shall be our labors," said a voice that was different from the first man. This one was pointed and hard like chipped flint. A voice that had a familiarity with authority, for the words had a boldness to them.

“Eternal shall be our reward,” replied the first man, his deep voice clouded by the mask he wore.

“Saracain is it?” said the second man, his question as pointed as the sharpened tip of a dart.

“Aye.”

“Why then have you summoned me here?”

“Where is the Master? It was he I was supposed to—” said Saracain. He was swiftly interrupted.

“He is away. That is all you need know.”

“And who are you?"

“That is none of your concern. All you need know is that I handle his affairs.” Then, there was a brief pause. “Did you ensure we are alone?”

“Aye.”

“Did you check the room above you?”

Another brief but tense pause. “We’re alone,” Saracain answered.

This made the other man quite irate, his words laced with malice as he responded. “Witless oaf! You have the audacity to summon me here, and have not the good sense to ensure that others—”

“You left me waitin’ here for two hours,” Saracain rumbled in an angry defense. “If there be spies above, they be more silent than mice. Ain’t heard a squeak or creak since I got here!”

Once more, silence reigned. Then the nameless man spoke. "If word spreads—"

"I'll check above when we're done," answered Saracain. This seemed to ease the fears among those gathered below.

"Get on with it then," commanded the nameless man.

"I got word of strangers pokin' about in Grainor. Some toe-headed lad askin' about for the woodsman that's been hole up at the Hale place."

"Tell me more."

"Well, I sent some boys over in the night to snatch 'em," Saracain said. "Naught but two returned."

"And the stranger?"

No answer from Saracain. Afterward, a long stillness grew, disturbed only by the shifting of feet in the dirt floor below. Then Saracain spoke up. "Of those that went to the farm only two returned, one of them bad off. So, my man had him…dispatched."

"The one that escaped? He said this stranger took down them boys like they was children. Had a sword and such with him. One of them blades that a lord or a soldier might carry."

"And this woodsman?"

"None of my men seen him about. I'm thinkin' he's still hole up with that farmer and his hounds," said Saracain. Then, after a long pause, he said, "What?"

“A man with flaxen hair, you say?”

“Yep. That’s `bout right.”

“Straight hair? Brown eyes?”

“Don’t know `bout them eyes,” said Saracain, his words letting the vulgar form of his rural accent slip through, “but his hair was a mess of curls. Neat, if my man spoke true. And young.”

Again, another long silence. One so tense that Herodiani could feel it through the wood of the floorboards.

“There’s a man in town seeking a meeting with the Master,” said the aide to the Master. “One who resembles the man you describe.”

“And?”

“I’ve already dispatched The Blade to attend to him.”

“And?”

“And nothing,” answered the nameless man, dismissively. “What else have you to report?”

“That’s it,” replied Saracain. “Thought the Master should be aware of what’s gone down as of late.”

The nameless man spoke again. “What is the name of this woodsman of whom you spoke.”

“Roe.”

“As I speak for the Master, my orders are thus—find this Roe and bring him to me.”

“And the farmer?”

“Leave them be.”

"What?" said Saracain, sounding confused. "Word of this is going to spread—"

"The Master desires the utmost secrecy in our work here," interrupted the nameless man. "Dead leasefolk raise uncomfortable questions and will demand action from the nobles. Better a rumor live than an inquiry." Then, he added, "Besides, word has come from the Master that the raids are to resume come the autumn. We will wait until then to attend to this Farmer Hale and his brood. Now, is there anything else to report?"

"No," said Saracain in a low voice.

"We are done here," said the nameless man hastily. "Bring me this Roe, and do not fail. Lest you too desire to join the ranks of the Legion Eternal."

There was some movement below as the light peeking through the floorboards dimmed, the two lamps now one. Then, Herodiani heard a third voice speak from the entrance of the tower. "And get your lumbering reed-hat ass up that ladder and check the room above."

Moving now to the southern window, the huntress peered out from the shadows. Her eyes followed the two men as they departed toward the trees from whence they came. Soon after, a low grumble rose from below as Saracain quietly cursed the pair of men well after they were out of earshot.

Herodiani repositioned herself back to the southeast corner of the tower once more, her sword and dagger in hand, beneath her Elanni cloak. She was invisible in the shadows that gathered in the gloom of that upper chamber. Her fingers flexed on the hilts of her sword and dagger as she waited.

The light of the lamp Saracain carried now shone up through the hole. Rungs creaked and groaned as the lumbering man ascended slowly. His soft grumbles and protests were ceaseless as he climbed.

Herodiani deduced that a possible encounter could resolve itself in one of two ways. Saracain would ascend, look around, and then quickly descend seeing nothing of note. Or he would see their things piled in the opposite corner and investigate. She silently prayed for the former. She prepared for the latter.

A hand thrust up from the opening, clutching a brass ring that held aloft a lamp. And with each rung that Saracain climbed, more light spilled into the room. Eventually, the head of the hooded man pushed up from the hole. With one more rung, Saracain's head and shoulders were now exposed.

As he paused to set the lamp on the floor of the second story, Herodiani rose to her feet slowly, making nary a sound as she did. Returning her dagger to the scabbard on her belt, she remained still, letting her cloak hide her from the dim light. Her brilliant blue eyes stared at the back of the mysterious man's head. It would have been so easy to dispatch him on that ladder, and perhaps that's what she should have done. Yet, there were rules and conditions to her involvement. Halsedric was very strict on these matters. If she had to take a life, it had to be done quickly, quietly. One misplaced thrust or errant strike and the resultant cries could call the others. She had to be patient and wait.

Huffing and puffing, the black-robed frame of the man so-named Saracain lifted himself from the ladder and stood erect in the upper chamber. He still hadn't seen her or even gazed in her direction. Breathless and heaving, he remained there for a time, the ladder seeming a greater impediment than the hill upon which the tower stood. Garbed head to toe in black, the leathery soles of his shoes scraped against rough and well-seasoned planks as he pivoted before bending down and taking up his lamp once more. Then he turned about again, letting the dim light of a single candle illuminate the room. The flame within the lamp flickered and sputtered, threatening to go out. Yet, in the blinking of an eye, the lamp recovered and shone once more.

The solitary candle cast a steady amber glow but had not the strength to reveal much. His deep hood screened the periphery of his vision, aiding the huntress in her task of remaining undetected. And as she stood there utterly still in the gloom of that corner, her hopes were raised that the eyes of the mortal would not be so keen or his curiosity so strong that he might just decide to descend and depart.

As he stood there, moving in a slow arc, she started to feel a wave of relief wash over her that this wish might come to fruition. No blood need be spilled this night. None of the complications that came with the taking of a life.

And then, Saracain took a step forward, heading directly to the northwest corner—the very same spot where their things lay. Halsedric's blade, his pack, and hers. That wave of relief was crushed and expunged with an anxious fervor that rushed through her veins. Her heart pounded, and her eyes fixed both cold and resolute on the form of Saracain as he took another step forward, then another as the light of his lamp started to reveal the blanket that covered their things.

They had been discovered. The die had been fatefully cast.

In an instant, the patient reserve of Herodiani's kin was gone, replaced by the huntress. Hard eyes now focused on her prey as she stealthily floated forward like a ghost in the room. There was no Saracain, no men outside the tower heading toward the forest. Only she and her prey.

Saracain stepped forward once more as Herodiani drew closer, both hands clutching her Elanni sword, the tip of it peeking out from beneath the bottom of her cloak. Close enough for a strike, she repositioned, the man's hood a perfect screen for her to do so. Her eyes fixed on the man as he stood there and inspected what the light of his lamp revealed. Then, with his right hand still holding the lamp, Saracain dug beneath his cloak. When he finally withdrew it, Herodiani could see the dull steel of a dagger reflected in the amber light. She knew now exactly what to do.

Withdrawing a half step, she clenched her teeth together and made a sharp hissing sound.

Hearing this, Saracain reacted immediately. He swung about, the blade of his dagger cutting the air, the tip of the weapon passing far and away from the hood of the huntress. And as he twirled about, the threat of his dagger passing her by, she lifted the shining steel of her sword. Her weapon flashed in the glow of the lamp as she stepped forward and lunged with her sword, her blade burying itself in the darkness of Saracain's hood. She felt the blade pierce vulnerable flesh, slicing its way in before the tip buried itself into hard bone. Here her thrust was stayed as the world around her slowed to a halt. With a single stroke, she had impaled the man through his throat, stifling any cry he might make and alerting his fellows.

For his part, Saracain stood there motionless, almost like a scarecrow in some farmer's field. One arm lifted high, still clutching the lamp, the other straight out, his meaty fingers grasping his dagger with a white-knuckle intensity. Herodiani's cut was so swift and precise, that the shock of it left the hooded man stunned, unable to move.

The huntress knew what was coming next. Her focus fixed on the lamp, she watched and waited for her victim to let go of the device. An act that happened almost as if it were rehearsed. With a deftness and speed that rivaled that of Halsedric, she let go of the blade, still gripping the hilt tightly with one hand, while the other reached out, and caught the ring on which the lamp hung.

The flame of the lamp sputtered and dimmed once more, the shadows of the pair twisting and dancing on the rough stone walls. Letting his dagger fall as well, the hands of Saracain instinctively reached for the steel of Herodiani's sword. His fingers vainly clutched about the weapon, the blade slicing his fingertips as they tried to pull the sharp steel that impaled him. And as he struggled, a thin stream of his blood began to run the length of her blade.

Lantern in hand, the huntress twisted the sword in the wound, causing her opponent to shudder, twitch, and groan hoarsely. Swiftly, she withdrew her blade before turning and stepping around her victim. Avoiding the window where they fought, Herodiani withdrew from the center of the room before finally setting the lamp down near the ladder. Once that was accomplished, she returned to finish her bloody business.

Saracain's hood fell back as his hands reached to cover the hole in his neck. He could not cry out. Only a rough wet noise was heard from him as he fell to his knees.

Setting her legs apart for a solid footing, the huntress raised her blade. With a swift and merciless slash, she ended the life of this Saracain by burying the blade in his skull. The weapon made a soft whooshing sound as it cut the air, followed by a sharp thunk that reverberated through her hands as the skull of her victim absorbed the energy of that killing blow.

As the body of Saracain fell forward, she withdrew, letting the weight of the corpse aid her in pulling her weapon free. Dark blood soon spilled out from the grievous wound, pooling on the wooden slats of the floor and dripping down through the cracks. No sound came from the man, nor did he move or spasm, as might happen with such a wound. He was, indeed, dead. And that was all that mattered.

Stepping over the body, Herodiani took a chance and inched her head out the side of the southern window, checking to see if any witnesses saw what transpired. She then repeated this with the rest of the openings, seeing nothing but empty wilderness below and hearing naught but the normal sounds of night.

Returning to the body, she knelt next to him and used his cloak to clean her blade. Standing again, she returned the weapon to its sheath before stealthily making toward the ladder and the lamp. To continue the ruse, she took up the lamp and descended the ladder. Once at ground level, she blew on the flame of the candle and extinguished the lamp before ascending to the second story once more.

As she returned to the watch, the conversation she overheard between Saracain and his superior repeated over and over in her head. Halsedric was in grave peril, far graver than she had faced. And in the quiet of that night, she offered a silent prayer for his deliverance.

CHAPTER TEN

"WORD HAS IT, YOU SEEK A MEETING WITH LORD Karne," said the man sitting across from Halsedric.

"And who are you that you could arrange such a meeting?" Halsedric's fingers moved slowly around the handle of the mug that was half full of ale.

"Someone who knows Lord Karne well," answered the man.

There was something about the man and his manner that Halsedric felt was a bit off. It was only the second alehouse the warrior visited that day, and now, someone associated with Lord Karne had come, as if handed a gift by the Allfather himself. Someone all too willing to put a stranger in contact with this mysterious northerner that everyone had heard of, but few knew. A stranger with a narrow face and a toothy smile that had a certain malicious feel to it. Keen and eager eyes. Eyes that locked on Halsedric with a strange and impish stare, barely able to veil the hostility that lay behind it. His blonde hair was slicked and combed back, as was fashionable among the wealthy. He was a lean and lanky figure, Halsedric noting well-defined musculature exposed by a gap in his clean linen shirt. A thief, maybe? A ruffian, no doubt. Or perhaps a little of both. The cities were always rife with such characters, whom wealthy men often paid for protection or other less wholesome acts. The two other men who followed him into the tavern had that very same feel. Brown-haired brutes with predatory eyes, and blades hidden on their persons.

"Jesper, son of Jerob," said the stranger. "If you doubt me, feel free to ask about. My fealty to the House of Karne is no great secret."

"And what is it you do for the House of Karne?" Halsedric asked casually.

"Does it matter?"

"Any here can boast of knowing Lord Karne," answered Halsedric. "Even the man who cleans his chamber pot."

"Aye," Jesper said with a nod. "As anyone can claim to bring matters of great import to the master. In that, friend, we are equal."

"True," acknowledged Halsedric with a nod.

"I think the real question here is, who are you that Lord Karne would want to speak with you?" The man leaned forward, resting his elbows on the table.

Everything he did—his manner, his tone, and his appearance—screamed danger to Halsedric. All the more reason for Halsedric to be assured the man was genuine.

Halsedric's eyes lowered, his stare fixed on his mug as his fingers wrapped about the handle. He had been to many alehouses in his time. They were mostly the same—dark, malodorous, and typically filled with the sorts of people most good folk studiously avoid. Poor quality ale and even poorer quality fare.

This establishment differed. The room was open, a half-wall defining the exterior. Light and noise from the street could come in, and the stagnant air could flow out to the city beyond. Yet, an open-air tavern was a mixed blessing. Cities tended to lack fresh, clean air. Whether it was horses, the unwashed stink of travelers and laborers, or offal washed into the gutters and alleyways, urban climes often had a reek to them that Halsedric bore with hidden disdain.

Slowly, Halsedric answered the man. "I represent certain interests—"

"What kind of interests?" interrupted Halsedric's inquisitor.

"Men who traffic in rare items." Halsedric paused. "From the East."

"A jobber, then," Jesper said quickly, the hint of derision in his words. "What kinds of things?" His stare never broke from Halsedric. The man rarely seemed to blink.

On this, Halsedric paused and looked at his mug once more, being coy with his response. "Rugs."

"Rugs?" mocked the man. "I assure you, Lord Karne has no problem finding fine rugs for reasonable coin."

"They are unique rugs.

"Oh? How so?"

"They are of a rare hue."

"Hue?"

"Color," answered Halsedric, the lids of his eyes narrowing.

The man's smile widened, though he no longer tried to hide his contempt for Halsedric. "And what color is that, friend?"

Once more, Halsedric delayed his answer. His eyes flashed upward, staring back at the man with greasy combed-back hair. "Black," he said after a time.

A flicker of doubt came and went as Jesper blinked. It was subtle, but to Halsedric, it was enough. A seed had been planted.

Black Tar was a rare commodity, often used for illicit purposes. While physicians employed it to alleviate pain and suffering, it was highly addictive. For some, mainly the wealthy and well-to-do, its addictive qualities were a fashionable diversion. For the poor, however, it was a means to control them. Making one an addict to Black Tar was to make one a slave whose chains were invisible. Shackles that bound men from within, not without. Thus, its use was highly restricted, if not prohibited outright. A highly profitable product for those less interested in the welfare of their fellow man than the profits it could yield.

For Halsedric's part, it was a gamble that this Karne was involved in illicit trading. A gamble that, despite Jesper's manner, seemed to yield results.

His voice suddenly lowered, Jesper answered, "I'm afraid that Lord Karne does not deal in obscure items such as this. And whomever it was that told you—"

"Very well," interrupted Halsedric. His eyes lowered quickly, and his fingers went from being wrapped around the handle of his mug to pressing against its base, moving it away from him. Pushing back from his chair, he leaned over and clutched the fabric of his cloak that rested on the ground next to him. "I see I was misled. No matter."

Tucking the mass of his cloak under his arm, Halsedric looked up and flashed a brief smile. "Offer my gratitude to your master for our meeting. I need to be away now." Exchanging a quick glance with the man before him, he saw shock overcome Jesper's expression.

As Halsedric rose, Jesper reached over and clutched his hand. "Don't be so hasty, friend."

Pausing for a moment, Halsedric looked down, then lowered back into his seat. Soon after, Jesper relaxed his grip and pulled away his hand.

Setting his cloak back onto the filthy dirt floor of the alehouse, Halsedric pulled his seat closer to the table. Once more, his fingers took the handle of his mug and set it down closer to him.

Jesper leaned closer. "I can arrange a meeting with Lord Karne, if that is your desire." His voice was low as he made the offer, and his confident grin returned.

Halsedric took a sip of the sweet and bitter ale from his glazed earthen mug. He was not quick to answer, taking his time to consider his options. Slowly, carefully, he set his cup back on the table.

"When?" Even before he asked the question, Halsedric knew something was amiss. This was *too* easy. Still, he had to take the risk.

Suspiciously looking both ways, Jesper lowered his voice further before answering. "Now, if you so wish."

"You must know Lord Karne well."

"Well enough," said Jesper. In an instant, the mocking face of the man turned stone serious as he continued, his voice near a low growl. "But I warn you, friend, if this be a ruse, you'll not be leaving Lord Karne's presence alive, if'n you know what I mean. Lord Karne is not a man to be trifled with."

Casually, Halsedric slid his mug to one side before leaning in, meeting Jesper's menacing scowl with one of his own. "Neither is He who sent me."

For a moment, Jesper's glowering stare fell, the man looking dumbfounded if not a little intimidated. The threat was received, though he did not understand the true meaning of Halsedric's words.

Jesper's demeanor then shifted. Gone was the open show of doubt and weakness. What returned was the slick vile thing that hid behind those insincere blue irises. It slowly crept back in as he pulled away and answered, "Of course. We all serve a master of some sort, do we not?"

"Some masters are greater than others." Halsedric's gaze bore down hard on Jesper.

The emissary of Karne merely shrugged, though in doing so, he avoided the gaze of the holy warrior. "Well, then," Jesper said after a moment, "best get to it." He lifted himself straight, the back of his legs pushing against the chair on which he sat. "Lord Karne is a busy man. I will take you to see him."

"Now?"

"Aye." Jesper nodded, that malicious smile of his vanishing. "It's now or never friend. If'n it's rugs you wish to sell. That's why I was sent, after all."

"This is highly irregular."

"It is how Lord Karne does his business," Jesper countered. "You either come now, or there will be no meeting...*friend.*" To Halsedric, the final word in that statement felt as if it had no place in Jesper's vocabulary.

Halsedric answered with an irritated stare and a sigh that carried with it the hint of a growl. Taking the handle of his mug, he lifted the ale to his lips, nearly emptying the contents within. The bottom of the earthenware container landed with a discontented thump as Halsedric set it back down. Gathering the cloak in his hands once more, he used the fringe of the garment to dry his lips and chin. The stale smell of earth and the elements invaded his nostrils, though it was thankfully brief. With a rustle of leathery soles shifting on hard dirt, Halsedric rose to meet his newfound guide.

Jesper motioned to the exit. "After you, friend."

"Are you not the guide?" replied Halsedric with a serious stare.

The corners of Jesper's lips relaxed, his mocking grin not as profound as before. "As you wish," he muttered.

Halsedric was never one much for the cities of men. He was raised on an estate. When he and his siblings were not under the instruction of learned tutors, they often had room to run and play. Forests. Gardens. Open meadows, and the tilled fields of the nearby farm folk. Fishing in the streams. Playing soldier with sticks as swords. Tending to horses in the stables. The world he knew was open and green, sounding and smelling of all things pastoral.

The cities of men were anathema to his understanding of the world. Cramped humanity living in meager dwellings. The noise and the smoke. Narrow roads clogged with moving forms. Anonymous shouting punctuated the low rumble of humanity. Foul smells permeated the very stone of the walls, sometimes wafting in and vanishing, and often surrounding him like a wretched fog. Ditches where rancid water ran down streets, and rotting food oft discarded in the alleyways.

There wasn't much spoken between Jesper and Halsedric as they traversed the maze of streets and alleyways of the walled city, the place a confusing mass of avenues both wide and narrow. The open streets and populations contained within a ruse of security, knowing that among the throng, thieves and urchins roamed. The alleys had a certain sincerity to them being relatively quiet and lonely. Further in, however, they turned claustrophobic and dark. Any solitude they may have offered quickly became tainted by the realization that they could be a prime setting for an ambush.

As they approached an intersection of one such alleyway, Halsedric noticed he was suddenly alone, Jesper having stopped several paces back. He slowed his pace, then stopped as two men appeared from each side of the intersecting lane. In a darkened, deserted path between high buildings, the warrior quickly determined that he had walked headlong into a trap. His head bowed as he clutched the cloak tucked under his arm. Tossing the garment aside, he turned about to face Jesper, heedlessly turning his back on the men slowly approaching from behind. The very same men that escorted Jesper to the alehouse. Men who had departed earlier in the conversation while Jesper kept his victim occupied. A tiny but salient detail that Halsedric had overlooked and one he would later chide himself for. But not now.

Several paces away, Jesper reached down and pulled a dagger from a sheath affixed to his belt. His fingers wrapped tightly about the hilt as he held the blade low.

"Did you truly think I'd believe you were sellin' Tar?" That malicious, toothy smirk grew again on Jesper's face as he stood there confidently.

Halsedric inhaled deeply and let out a despondent sigh. He turned slightly to look over his shoulder at the men who approached from his rear. Some distance behind where he stood, the faint hiss of a blade being drawn quietly echoed off the stone walls that bordered the lonely alley. At once, Halsedric began to undo the buttons of his vest.

When Halsedric was nearly halfway through unbuttoning his vest, Jesper said, "What you doin'?"

As he started to undo the final button, Halsedric replied, “Removing my vest.”

The smirk faded from Jesper’s face as he looked on, befuddled by Halsedric’s casual behavior. “What?”

Pulling the garment free of one arm, Halsedric moved casually to remove the leather vest before holding it before him. The vest was new, mottled only in a few spots and free from the many patches and repairs of its previous counterpart.

Lazily tossing the vest on the heap of his cloak, Halsedric turned to the men behind him before pivoting back to Jesper.

Flaring his arms and shrugging his shoulders, Halsedric said, “The vest is new. If it remains on my person, I will most likely need to patch it, and that will not do. After all, I may need something to cover all the blood on my shirt when I am done here.”

CHAPTER ELEVEN

HALSEDRIC LOOSENED HIS GRIP ON JESPER'S vest, letting the body of the battered thug crumple to the ground. The mocking blue eyes of Halsedric's attacker were closed now, his face mangled and covered in his own blood. As the motionless flesh collected in a heap at his feet, Halsedric noticed the hilt of his attacker's dagger sticking out from his abdomen. The blade had found a tender area just below his breast, the wrapped leather of the hilt poking out from the white linen of his shirt. Blood began to seep into the linen and surrounded the wound, the blade having dug deep into Halsedric's flesh and vitals.

Barely above the din of the streets beyond, Halsedric heard the clink and clank of metal hitting the stone alley of the cramped avenue. Looking up, he saw the form of a man standing there, legs slightly apart. A familiar face with dark hair and dark eyes that gazed at him in stunned amazement. With a mouth hanging open in shock, surrounded by a shaggy beard, Roe's face said it all. The trapper had a hard time believing his eyes.

It took Halsedric a moment before he recognized Roe, calling the trapper by name.

Roe was as motionless as a statue. The trapper's eyes fixed on the handle of the blade that protruded from Halsedric's abdomen.

Halsedric called out again, this time with a slight smile. "Roe?"

Stepping around the downed form of Jesper, Halsedric drew near to the befuddled trapper. "Roe? Are you well?"

Dumbly, his hand shaking, the trapper pointed to the handle of the dagger protruding out from Halsedric's lower chest. Roe's lips moved, but naught but a squeak issued from his mouth.

Only now was Halsedric cognizant of the blade wedged between his bones, the tip of it sending a sharp cold pain through his body as he moved. With a grunt, he reached up with his left hand, wrapped his fingers about the handle, and wrenched the dagger from his body in a single swift pull. From his lips escaped a breathy grunt, the sucking wound in his flesh affecting his lung. With one hand pressed against the wound, he stared momentarily at the grayish blade, streaked with his own crimson blood. He murmured, disgusted, "And this was a new shirt."

Being stabbed was nothing new to the holy warrior. The first wound he suffered was the worst, though time and conflict had desensitized him. Halsedric cast the blade aside with a scowl.

"How?" The words spilled out from Roe's mouth.

Halsedric took a moment to look around the scene of battle. Three bodies lay in the street, two in close proximity to one another, the other lying face up, sprawled out on the lane. It all happened so fast, as was typical of such encounters. Two approached from behind, blades drawn. Their slow aggressive strides had underscored their supreme confidence in the superiority of their numbers.

Halsedric, however, was not someone who could be so easily slain. The first went down when Halsedric connected with a single blow to the side of the man's head. He could feel something break beneath the flesh of his assailant as he landed the blow, his fist connecting with a nauseatingly wet thump. The other ruffian came in from the side. Halsedric was quicker. Parrying the incoming thrust with his arm, he managed to lay hold of the man by his clothes, pulling him in close and sending a knee to his groin. The warrior remembered a distinctly strained squawk from his attacker as the man's eyes bulged, his face lighting up like potent liquor cast on greedy flames. Not a fatal strike in the least, though debilitating enough. After his attacker fell, the man no longer moved or groaned.

Ever the cunning leader, Jesper had waited until the others engaged before he went in for his piece of the kill. His first and only strike landed as Halsedric turned about, having finished with the two other ruffians. Jesper's face lit up with a broad and sadistic grin as he stuck the warrior, thrusting the blade in with all his might. A smile that faded quickly, unable to understand why Halsedric seemed so indifferent to the debilitating blow. A regrettable pause for which Jesper paid dearly.

Grabbing tight the hem of Jesper's vest, Halsedric sent a volley of blows to the face of the vain and wicked man. A pummeling retort that shattered bone and split flesh. Was it four blows, or five? Halsedric had lost count in the heat of the moment. Yet, when the last blow was struck, Jesper's head swayed and weaved like the lifeless gob of a scarecrow, the will that drove muscle and sinew lost with the swift embrace of unconsciousness or death.

At the very least, he didn't get stuck from behind this time around. No need to chastise himself for leaving his back exposed.

All that was now in the past. Whether Jesper still lived or not, Halsedric did not care.

The man with the slick smile ceased to be a threat, though his parting gift was a sucking wound in the warrior's abdomen.

As Roe stood there transfixed and dumbfounded, a single solitary figure appeared at the entrance of the alley. No doubt some nameless city dweller, pausing for a moment to stop and wonder what was afoot in the shaded avenue.

"Roe." Halsedric's wheezing voice was commanding. When the trapper did not acknowledge his call, Halsedric shouted again. "Roe!"

As if shaken from a dream, Roe looked up at Halsedric, his face still flooded with confusion, his eyes wide and filled with fear.

"Are…are you hurt?" Roe asked.

Halsedric looked briefly down at the wound, now covered by his hand. "Yes," he said with cool composure. "Now, if you would be so inclined, I will need your assistance to gather my things."

Still stunned, Roe did not move. Behind him, a second figure stopped, turning to look at the scene.

Halsedric grew impatient and had the impulse to bark out to Roe again. Leaning to one side, the warrior stared curiously at the meager gathering of bystanders, taking a moment of his own to ponder his next actions.

"Roe!" Halsedric barked, his tone having a distinct urgency to it. It was enough to finally shake the trapper from his stupor.

Finally having Roe's full attention, Halsedric pointed with his free hand at the entrance of the alley some paces away. A wordless signal that finally made the trapper react. Roe craned his neck about momentarily before turning in full.

Once he spied the pair of observers at the entry of the lane, Roe immediately made two quick strides toward the gathering bystanders. Hand waving in the air, he shouted at the onlookers, "Get off, you lot! Lessin' you're looking for trouble and worse!"

Their curiosity suddenly lessened by threatening words, the pair of men dispersed, one walking off quickly, the other darting off in a clumsy dash. Roe slowed his gait, then stopped, watching the people pass by on the street, ensuring that no one else was willing to dare a glance.

Halsedric winced as he reached down and grabbed the lifeless arm of Jesper, dragging him like a child's doll while his other hand covered the gash in his gut.

Assured that no one else was watching, Roe spun about and walked quickly back to Halsedric. Marching with a purposeful gait, he muttered something beneath his breath. He paused briefly as he spied the dagger he dropped earlier. There he paused and promptly plucked his weapon from the ground before slotting it purposefully into the holder on his belt. When he approached Halsedric, he acted without needing instruction, laying hands on the prone form of one of the other ruffians. With a labored grunt, he dragged the limp body of the man to a nearby threshold. With haste, he pulled the man's body to the recess to partially hide whatever evidence remained of the fight.

Halsedric followed Roe's lead, pulling Jesper out of the narrow street to the threshold. With a growl and grimace, he let go of Jesper before reaching down and grabbing him by his vest. Lifting him off of the ground like a child's toy, he tossed the thug atop one of his minions that already lay in the doorway.

Eyes transfixed by Halsedric's unearthly strength, Roe paused for a moment as he dragged the third and last of Halsedric's attackers to the doorway. As he neared, Roe mumbled dumbly, "How can this be?"

"Make your inquiries later," Halsedric wheezed before pointing behind him with his free hand. "Take my cloak and vest."

"Aye," Roe answered as he dropped his load at the threshold before bending down and rolling the man into the niche. Once done, he raced to gather Halsedric's things.

While Roe was preoccupied, Halsedric knelt down next to the pile of his fallen assailants and drew his dagger from its sheath. Air sucked in and out from the gash in his abdomen as he cut a wide patch of cloth from the trousers of one of the fallen attackers. From another, he cut off the sleeve. One of the men moved and groaned, Halsedric unsure as to which. Wincing as he stood, he gripped the cloth remnants in his hand while stuffing his dagger back into his sheath.

"What are you doin'?" Roe looked on at the scene, in one hand the brown and patched leather vest, and draped over his arm, the heavy woolen cloth of Halsedric's cloak.

"Something to pad the wound until it has healed," remarked Halsedric as he turned. Looking up towards the darkened intersection, he added, "Let us retire to a place that will hide us from spying eyes."

As Roe grabbed the cloth fragments from Halsedric's hands, the warrior pointed to an intersection farther down in the lane. "Over there," he said, gasping.

Dashing around the corner, the pair set about patching Halsedric's wound. Roe wadded the wool into a crude bandage, handing it to Halsedric, who pressed it against the cut. Then, withdrawing his dagger once more, the trapper started to cut the fragment of the sleeve Halsedric took from one of his attackers into crude strips. As he labored, Roe managed a quick glance at the crimson stain growing on Halsedric's white linen shirt. "That looks bad," he remarked.

"No worse than any of the others," answered the warrior. With a frown, he grumbled, "This was a new shirt."

"A big enough stain that a guard is gonna notice," said Roe, his blade crudely cutting the linen cloth, rending about as many fibers of the weave as he was slicing.

"It will be hidden by a vest and cloak."

"A guard may notice."

"That is my concern," answered Halsedric, his tone turning impatient. Changing the subject, he then asked, "Why are you here in the city?"

"I might ask the same of you," answered Roe, somewhat distracted by his work.

"I was establishing a meeting with this Lord Karne."

"Were you now?" answered Roe as he paused. Puzzled and slightly amused, he added, "No one meets with this Karne."

"A lesson learned with some pain," remarked Halsedric. Noticing that Roe had paused his work, Halsedric impatiently cleared his throat.

"Right," muttered Roe, as he returned to cutting strips. Once the sleeve was divided, he set his dagger back into its sheath and went about knotting the strips together. "Where's the maid?"

"Waiting outside the city," answered Halsedric. "Why are you here?"

"Visiting Karne."

It wasn't until he was done that Roe looked up and noticed the intense gaze that Halsedric cast his way. Visibly shocked by the stare, Roe asked low, "What?"

"To what end?" Halsedric's face flushed.

It took a moment for Roe to interpret the meaning of the warrior's question. "It's not like that. I snuck into his house and looked about a bit. That's all."

"How?"

Holding the completed bandage together, Roe held it out, inspecting its full length. "Didn't I say I was once a thief?"

"You said you were a street urchin."

"Urchins steal. Don't matter if'n it be a purse or a sausage or two from a nobleman's pantry."

Lifting his arms, Halsedric winced as Roe went about wrapping the strips around his abdomen, securing the padding in place. As he worked, Roe muttered, "This ain't gonna hold."

"You made your disgust in me quite clear."

"Aye." Roe nodded enthusiastically. "I had spent that night and day next headin' back to the Hale house, takin' paths I was hopin' you couldn't follow. But the night after, I had a dream."

"What kind of dream?"

"The kind you don't forget," Roe said softly. "The kind where you wake up screamin' into the night. One where a messenger of the Divine comes and tells you to go back."

As Roe tied off the bandage, Halsedric could feel the various knots in the wrappings press against his flesh. A discomfort he would have to bear for now. As Roe stepped back, he let go of the ends of the linen strip and examined his work. "That ain't gonna hold long," he grumbled.

Lowering his arms, Halsedric pointed to his things lying on the street. "Help me with the vest and cloak. The vest will aid in keeping the bandage in place."

Roe bent down, retrieving the vest first. Holding the garment open so that Halsedric could put his arms through, Roe continued his tale. "He told me to seek out the Karne estate, then find you. So, I did. Then I saw you leavin' the alehouse with Jesper. So, I followed."

The leather of the vest creaked as it was stretched over the bulk of bandages. Each button strained against taut tanned hide. "I lost you there for a bit," Roe continued. "And when I found you again, you were beatin' that man hard. Then I noticed the dagger stickin' from your gut."

With the vest fastened all the way up, a small patch of crimson showed past the lapel. Pulling it tight at the fringe, Halsedric remarked in a strained tone of voice "That will do. Now the cloak."

Bending down to retrieve the cloak, Roe said. "How is it a man can be stuck in the gut and—"

“Part of my condition. Did you discover anything about Karne?”

“Aye,” said Roe with a nod as he straightened. “First things first though. We need to be out of here and right quick before the mess you made is found.”

“How?” Halsedric said as Roe helped him on with his cloak.

“I can take you unseen to a spot near the gate. You’ll have to make your way out from there. I need to get my mounts from the stables. I can’t track you much outside the city. Where’s your camp?”

“A watch tower near a league north of the main gate.”

“That place?” Roe broke away and pressed himself up against the wall before peering around the corner. It only took a moment before he pulled back. “Aye, I know where it is. I’ll find you.” With urgency, he added, “Now, we need to be gone from here. Someone’s comin’ down the alley, and we’ll be pinched for sure if we hang about here much longer.”

CHAPTER
TWELVE

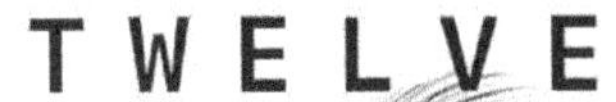

THEIR ESCAPE FROM THE CITY WAS CLEAN, BOTH men cleaning the blood from their hands at a back-alley basin where spring water collected and spilled into a gutter. No guard bothered to question Roe. Halsedric mingled with a group of travelers departing the city, the mass of humanity providing a fine cover to get him past the city gates. After that, it was a short walk for both men past the outer dwellings and into the wilds beyond. Only after they reached the tower and Herodiani gave them the sign to approach, did they set about cleaning and binding the warrior's wound properly.

"Do you always travel with ample cloth for bindin' wounds?" asked the trapper as he knotted the end of the bandage over the wound.

Halsedric let out a grunt as Roe tied off the bandage wrappings across his abdomen. His face pinched with pain, he stared down at the wrappings, his crimson blood seeping into the cloth. "Always. It is a hazard of the calling." Still cinched around his waist by a belt, his shirt was splayed out on the grassy ground, the lower portion of it tucked in his trousers. The cool stone of the tower walls braced the warrior's back. Reaching over to pick up the loose cloth of his shirt he examined the section that was split by the thug's knife, now marked by the dark remains of blood. Halsedric shook his head gently in disgust before allowing the cloth to fall back to the ground. Not all the blood on the shirt had dried, for afterward he spied wet crimson stains on his fingertips. These he ran through a matted patch of grass to clean away the blood.

"You know that dead body in there? Someone's gonna come looking for him," said Roe of the man that Herodiani had slain the night before.

"That does not concern me," answered Halsedric, testing the wrappings. "A fine dressing," he added.

One of the horses snorted nearby, the beasts milling about on the northern side of the tower. Roe lifted one knee and rested his arm on it, placing the other on his hip. As Halsedric started to dress, Roe stared intently at the wound before turning his head to the south and scanning the horizon. "We should be away from here, and right quick. You picked a fine spot to be seen from a furlong or more. And, they says that—"

"This is a fell and haunted place?" Halsedric was quick to interrupt.

Roe's head tilted to one side. "Aye. And how'd you know that?"

"Painted markings inside," answered Halsedric. "Hidden. Either with purpose or by the passing of time. Whether dark rites were performed here or not, I suspect enough rumors and tales were spread to dissuade the curious and wary."

"Either way, we need to be gone."

"Where shall we go?"

This time, turning his head northwards, Roe scanned the landscape. "I know a few folk in these parts where we can shelter ere the night comes. Then we strike out before the dawn. Let that wound of yours—"

"My wound is of little concern," Halsedric cut in with a note of urgency. Partially preoccupied with tying his shirt closed, he went on. "Who was this man that you claimed could tell us more of the Wychwood?"

"Aye, Gallain?" Roe's attention shifted back to his wounded companion. "He's days away. Mayhaps seven days from where we set, if'n we ride dawn to dusk. Mayhaps six. Then there's a matter of us leavin' our things at Hale's farm."

"Do you think we can be at the homestead of Farmer Hale before dawn if we ride night and day?"

"Two, most like," said Roe with a tepid nod. "But, even with the moon and stars, it gets mighty dark in these parts."

"That is not much of a concern," answered Halsedric, tying the last cloth tie at the collar of his ruined shirt. "The Lenogala are tireless and can move at night. Herodiani can lead us."

Roe thumped the fingers of one hand against his chest in a show of concern. "I can't guide you in the dark."

"Are there streams ample enough to hide our passing?"

"Aye," answered Roe with a nod.

"Can we travel to them ere nightfall?"

"Aye. But even if'n your beasts need no rest, mine does," Roe said, motioning to the silvery white Lenogala that grazed nearby.

With one hand up, Halsedric signaled Roe to silence. "Your beast will have time to rest. My greater concern is if we are pursued. We risk more unwelcomed attention drawn to the house of Farmer Hale." He paused for a moment, remarking, "We have created trouble enough."

"Aye," answered Roe with an amicable nod. "Agreed. I know a few paths that'll throw them off our trail. But, we may not get there ere dawn, that'll be for sure."

Roe looked away for a moment, seemingly collecting his thoughts. Then his attention fixed once more on Halsedric as he went on. "If'n we avoid the villages and stick to folk I knows is belivin' types, I'm thinking we can approach ol' Hale's place without much notice, savin' his hounds and such. We rest there for a spell, then head out to Gallain's 'stead the night next, if'n that's what you want."

"That is acceptable," said Halsedric after a moment's consideration.

"Aye," said Roe in agreement. "So, I'll start makin' ready to leave?"

"Not just yet," replied Halsedric.

"We can't be seen sittin' here all day," protested Roe.

"What did you discover about Karne?"

Roe's brow furrowed for a moment before the confusion lifted. "Oh, that!" With a clever smile, he softly said, "My little visit."

"Yes," Halsedric answered with impatient eyes.

"Well, he ain't there, for one. Been gone for some time now."

Halsedric's lids narrowed, his ire visibly showing.

In an instant, Roe's eyes lit up. "Oh, and this!" Roe started to slide his hand beneath his vest, though he stopped and momentarily looked at his blood-stained fingers. Fearful he would mar the document he carried, he ran his open palms vigorously against his trousers before attempting a second time. The weathered leather of his vest bulged as his hand dug beneath. Soon after, he produced a folded parchment, dog-eared in one corner and wrinkled. Pinching the document between two fingers, Roe held the prize out for Halsedric.

For his part, Halsedric took the document and unfolded it, revealing what was contained within.

"He's got a mighty fine desk, that Karne," Roe said as Halsedric scanned the contents on the tanned paper. "I found that in an empty drawer. Don't know what it means, though. I ain't much for writin', though I knows a few letters and all. Ain't seen nothing like that."

Laid out on the parchment was a square comprised of symbols, each geometrical in their form. Some were circles, while others were squares with interiors filled, half-filled, or not filled at all.

"It is a cipher," said Halsedric as his eyes scanned the scrawls. "Though the details of it, I know naught."

"How'd you know?"

"Such ciphers were used to great effect in the war," answered the wounded warrior as he continued to study the page.

With a note of curiosity, Roe asked, "What war?"

Halsedric offered the trapper a knowing glare. A look that took Roe a moment to recall why it was they parted company. Talk of the war of the prophets and the revelation that made him angry enough to leave. "Oh," muttered the trapper. "Right."

Lifting the fingers of one hand from the parchment, Halsedric noticed red stains left behind from the pads of his fingers. His lips taut and grumbling his annoyance, he set about wiping the offending hand on his trousers before using it again to fold the parchment. Holding the letter up like a prize, his discontent faded, Halsedric said, "This may yet be of use. I have studied the subject of ciphers while wintering in Elenur."

One brow arched as Roe said, "You study such things? Winterin'?"

"The Elanni are gracious hosts. Lord Aurogeloi has an extensive collection of books and scrolls. Though I may have duties to attend while I am there, I am still afforded some leisure time."

Halsedric pondered for a time, then looked to Roe again. "Any other such prizes?"

"No," answered Roe with a shake of his head. "Didn't want to press what luck I had. Though, I'll say that I heard a couple of Karne's toughs drinkin'. They said Karne's been gone for a bit and might not be back too soon. Didn't say where, tho." Roe took a moment to search his thoughts before adding, "And that's it."

"Very well," Halsedric said dispassionately. Turning his head to the side, he gazed over at the doorway. "We should investigate what transpired here while we were in the city."

Hand out, Roe offered assistance to Halsedric, who accepted. Though, as Halsedric rose, Roe winced. The warrior's grip like that of a vice. As the trapper flapped up his sore fingers, Halsedric flashed a shamefaced smile. "Apologies," he muttered.

Roe remained outside while Halsedric stepped into the tower. His eyes immediately discovered the large dark spot on the dirt floor. Head following an unseen line to the rafters, he witnessed the stains where blood had seeped through the narrow gaps in the floorboards. Also outlined by the light that shone into the second story of that tower was the dark form from whence the crimson fluid came. Near the southern arrow slit, the bird of blue and orange plumage that had followed them was perched at the edge of a stone shelf, its glossy black eyes watching the warrior while it chirped.

As the warrior began to ascend the ladder, the trapper followed after him, stepping into the interior of the tower, still waggling his hand in the air. The wood of the rungs groaned beneath the weight of the warrior as his boots scuffed the grain. With each rung ascended, Halsedric winced, the activity triggering a sharp pain as he lifted his arms.

The wood of the floor groaned softly as Halsedric exited the ladder and approached the dead body of the man named Saracain. By now, his skin was pale, his flesh cold, and no doubt the body stiff. Herodiani knelt by the southern window, the hood of her cloak back and her bow at the ready. Halsedric drew close and knelt at the prone body.

Face down, the dead man lay at the very spot where he was slain, his hands tucked beneath his throat. Halsedric knelt and flipped the body over, grunting slightly as he did, inflaming his wound again. The cadaver had gone stiff, rigor having set in.

Roe came alongside as Halsedric shuffled forward a bit and took a position near the dead man's head. Pulling back the hood, he then proceeded to tear the mask of black cloth that covered most of his face. Blood had dried in the black mane of the deceased and even left short tracks along his forehead as it ran along the skin. As the cloth was ripped away, the body twitched slightly as if life existed once more. But Saracain was dead. Dead and gone. Halsedric tossed the rent cloth aside.

Looking long at his face, Halsedric tried to imagine what the man looked like when he was still breathing. The wound that cleaved the top of the head and the effusions of blood along the face and crown made it difficult to discern. His face, while long, was fleshy, with jowls forming at the chin. Clean-shaven, his mouth hung open, dried blood having collected along the lips and chin.

"Saracain, you say?" Roe sounded dubious.

"That was his name, yes," replied Herodiani.

Halsedric tilted his head slightly and offered Roe a sidelong look. "Why do you ask?"

Roe shrugged his shoulders before answering. "Well, If'n I reckon correct, his name ain't Saracain. It's Malto. Son of Malvo, a butcher in Grainor. He's a tax collector. Lives not far from the village."

Roe sniffed, then rubbed his hand under his nose. "A right pig of a man. Lives well off the sweat of others. I ain't forgot when he took them goats from the widow of a farmer named Renard. Slew one of them and had a feast with his friends. Gave away another. The rest he sold to pay her debt. A few of the folk from the village bought the goats and gave them back to the widow."

"There was another whose name was spoken," piped up Herodiani. "They named him the Master."

"And what of him?" said Halsedric.

"They said he was away. And that the other man who was at the meeting was attending to his affairs."

Halsedric turned his head more and looked at Roe, whose gaze met that of the warrior. It was clear by the look in Roe's eyes that they were both thinking the same thing. The person referred to as The Master was, most likely, Lord Karne.

"Why the name?" said Roe after a moment. "And the mask. If'n they knew each other, why hide it?"

"That I cannot answer," said Halsedric as he lifted from the ground. "What I can say is that we need to be away, and with haste."

"What about him?" responded Roe, lazily pointing at the corpse. "If'n folk be meetin' here, someone's gonna notice a dead man when he starts to puff up and stink."

Halsedric considered the remains of Malto for a moment, looking the dead man over as he pondered. "Leave him as he is. We need to leave this place and with haste. Perhaps by the time Malto, son of Malvo, is discovered, we will be too far away to pursue."

"You going to pray for him too?" said Roe, his concern audibly half-hearted. "Like you did for them that got killed in the barn?"

"Yes," nodded Halsedric as he moved to where his gear was piled. "I assure you I can ride and pray simultaneously. Now, let us depart."

CHAPTER THIRTEEN

WHILE THEIR RIDE TO THE CITY OF OREM WAS done at a leisurely pace, their flight dictated that they moved both night and day for nearly two days straight. Only when Roe protested did they finally halt and rest for the night. They eventually reached the Hale farm near the noontime hour, quickly making for the barn where they could unburden themselves for a time. Herodiani departed to meet with the wards that were requested to keep vigil over the lands of Farmer Hale. Halsedric concerned himself with removing the bandages he had been wearing over the course of several days.

His back against a pile of hay just inside the entrance of the barn, Halsedric started untying the laces of his shirt with a perplexed expression on his face. As his fingers picked at the knots, he spoke to Roe, who was with him in the barn. "What did the Prophet Wolland instruct you in your time together?"

"Many things," answered Roe, equally confused, as per his expression. "Why it's better to be kind than tough. Why love's better than lust. The teachings of them other prophets, both now and long ago."

"Yet, he did not tell you of the many prophecies spoken by his brethren? The select among men? Those chosen to carry the message of the Allfather to mortal ears?"

Roe hesitated before answering, not quite sure what to say. "Well, to be fair, he was tendin' to them that was lost in the cold stone of the city. Ain't much care had by folks cold and starvin' on the street to hear about prophecy and all. If'n you're bringing such folk to a new life, best to speak about things that matter to them."

As he listened to the trapper talk, Halsedric paused his activity, giving Roe his full attention. "This is true," he said as he resumed undoing each tie. "Our purpose here, our mission, stems from a conflict that is ages old. A flame lit long before men came out of the East. There are many powers in this world, all endowed with life by the Divine. The Elanni, of course. Wizards. Heralds, with whom I converse with and serve. A great host, both spirit and flesh."

Halsedric paused, and his head lifted slightly. Casting a glance at Roe, he continued. "Yet, not all have remained true to their maker's will. There are those who have strayed, severing the bond of love and loyalty to their Maker, opposing Him in open rebellion."

"How many are there?" inquired Roe in a soft and nervous voice.

"Many," answered Halsedric, slipping out of his shirt. He let the upper portion fall to the ground before picking at the knot that held the bandages around his chest. The trapper had bound the ends quite firmly, making it difficult to pull one end loose. "Ancient texts that survive from those elder days speak of this rebellion originating in the east."

Frustrated, as he continued to pick and pry the knot, Halsedric paused for a moment and exhaled his discontent. Roe saw this, and remarked, "You're strong. Just rip them off."

Halsedric was unamused. "A goodly supply of bandages is a welcome thing." At once, he looked down at the ground, his eyes searching for his belt and the knife that it held. Retrieving the knife, he set the blade into the top strip of cloth. With a single cut, the bandage fell away, the keen edge of the blade separating the woven cotton fibers almost noiselessly. As the ends hung down, he leaned forward and returned the blade to its sheath.

Taking one of the cut ends of the bandages, he sat forward and tried to untangle himself, rather unsuccessfully. Reaching behind was awkward, and he had a hard time transferring the end of the bandage from one hand to the other.

Roe saw his companion's frustration building. "Aye, let me get that," he said as he scrambled to his feet. Pacing over to where Halsedric sat, the trapper knelt at the warrior's side. Hay and dirt ground beneath the soft heels of his hide boots as he did.

Halsedric handed Roe one cut end of the long bandage before sitting forward, lifting his arms and letting the trapper untangle the rest. As Roe went about his task, Halsedric continued his explanation. "In time, the enemy would come to settle in the lands to the south of the Dragonspires. A place whose name is known from history and myth. Furlornur." He then turned his head to Roe and asked, "Have you heard of it?"

With a nod, Roe answered, "Aye. I've heard it a time or two."

"Many in number are these rebels. Yet among them, four are acknowledged to be the greatest of their kind."

Roe paused his work. "Wouldn't have anything to do with what them Cathars worship, would it?"

"Yes. The worship of The Four. Though it is not just Cathars who worship them. The Hakan as well. We know that many hold such beliefs and hide them from the eyes of the Faithful."

As the last strip sagged away from Halsedric's frame, the pad of cloth it held in place still stuck to the warrior's chest by a bond of dried blood. As Halsedric pried it away tenderly, he exposed something that made the trapper audibly gasp. Instead of a line of pink and swollen flesh cut across Halsedric's abdomen, the terrible remainder of Jesper's last treacherous stroke was clean flesh, unmarred, spattered with maroon patches of dried blood. The gash had healed at an uncanny rate, leaving Roe speechless and in awe.

"Did I not tell you of my condition?" remarked Halsedric, seeing the astonishment in Roe's eyes.

Roe's mouth twitched before speaking, as if the words struggled to make it past his aimless tongue. "Aye. But I weren't expectin' this."

"Touch it, if you so desire," said Halsedric. The words snapped Roe from his bewilderment, the trapper shaking his head, his eyes blinking rapidly as he pulled away.

As Roe lifted himself from the ground, Halsedric said, "Do not discard those bandages. We will need to have them cleaned should we need them again."

With little more than a grunt of acknowledgment from the trapper, Halsedric went about dressing once more. As Roe returned to his spot in the barn, Halsedric slipped his arms back into the sleeves of his shirt. "It was the Prophet Faylar who first wrote the prophecy concerning The Four—a Nolan, I might add. He was among the first prophets who arose in the midst of men. Through inspired writings, he details the rise of The Four, though by that time, the first of The Four had already been thrown down. The second, I fear, is now with us, though his presence remains unseen."

"How do you know?" said Roe, preoccupied with folding the bandages. "I mean, this be the first I've heard any of this, even in alehouse talk."

As he pulled his shirt about his frame, Halsedric leaned back against the hay once more. The straw squeaked and groaned as his weight pressed against it, the musty smell of the dried grass coming around him in a bloom. "The Great War was long ago. Long before the campaign against The Prophetess and her vile brood. The conflict itself was a terrible thing, nearly pushing both mortal and Ageless to the utter brink of destruction. Were it not for the intervention of the Heavenly Host, sent across the Western Sea, we would not be here. From that war, most of our present troubles stem. Yerch. Attin. Morgurs. The Black lands of Furlornur, where naught grows, save tortured things that bite and mar. It birthed the Sorrowing Sea where the dead lay, trapped forever in the icy embrace of the deeps."

"If'n these four were undone, why then did the second war come about?" said Roe, his labors slowing as he was drawn more into Halsedric's tale.

"For a time, there was peace," said Halsedric with a nod. "After the fall, the remaining host of the enemy was hunted. Those that remained sought sanctuary in distant and untamed places. Mountains. Wild lands. Places where neither mortal nor Ageless go. The Wodemen know more of their presence than we, as they have fought in many campaigns against the Yerch in ages past. Oft times you will discover such creatures in dark places, where evil is said to find sanctuary.

The host of the enemy was scattered and driven away. In time, the Elanni reclaimed their former dominions. As the world healed, the tribes of Men grew, spreading their numbers over the face of the earth, settling far afield in lands no longer afflicted by darkness. A tenuous peace was had. Few were the wars between tribes of men, and with an abundance of freedom, men prospered.

Yet not all had been overthrown. In time, even the Ageless grew less vigilant, presuming that whatever evil plagued this world was contained in distant, inhospitable places. In their inadvertency, a hidden malice grew. She who was so named the Prophetess."

Head down as if lost in thought, Halsedric went silent. Roe stared at him during this time, a question burning in the man's eyes. Not long after, as if his inquisitiveness could no longer be restrained, he asked, "You said a second evil has risen. Was this the Prophetess?"

As if shaken from a dream, Halsedric looked at Roe dumbly, mulling the question in his mind. "No," he answered at first, letting a silence linger afterward. He continued, "As we traveled in the Aranach, we came upon a pair of Yerch, one having slain the other."

His head bowed, Halsedric recalled once more the images of the Yerch they slew on their trek to the Horn of Torgiv. "Tell me, Roe, what do the peoples of these lands know of the Yerch?"

Roe's eyes widened for a moment, and his cheeks puffed as he exhaled noisily, ending in a soft whistle. "Well, now," he said, quite unsure what to say, "I mean, there's talk. They got horns and such, and folk always scarin' the little ones that the Yerch'll come for them if'n they don't go to bed. A farmer said some Yerch made off with a few of his hens some time back. And Ewers down near Boggy Deeps swears Yerch been stealin' his hogs. But he's been known to stretch the truth a bit. He likes to play the bones, if'n you know my meanin'. Them missin' hogs most like been lost to payin' his debts, seeing that ol' Lady Ewers might beat him with a pan if'n she finds he's been gamblin' again."

Roe paused before continuing. "But from what ol' Hale tells me, whatever got at them hens weren't no fox nor wolf. Tore up the shelter but good. Left bits of them birds in its flight. The tracks they left weren't no animal neither—they was boots. Somethin' upright and moving at a bit of a clip."

"How big were the tracks?"

"Didn't say," answered Roe. "Though I'd reckon if'n there'd be somethin' unnatural about them, someone would have said." He thought about the story a bit more, his eyes looking to the side as he did. "Don't know no man eatin' some bird raw... not even them bandits that used to trouble these parts. One of the farmers said he caught sight of one, and it had horns. That's when stories of Yerch started."

"What else did he say of these thieves aside from horns?"

"Like what?"

"Their eyes. What they wore. The color of their skin."

Roe shrugged his shoulders. "I don't reckon much else. Just tracks and horns."

With a frown on his face, Halsedric grumbled his frustration.

"Why you ask?" said Roe.

"The Yerch we encountered in the Aranach—they were quite different. One was sallow-skinned. The other, much darker. Broader. The Yerch of old were known to be pale and lean. This new creature..."

Ruminating on the images in his head, Halsedric paused for a moment. "It differed greatly. And it sported a strange mark on his brow," he added, tapping the center of his forehead with his finger.

"Meanin' what?"

"Each and every foul perversion of The Four was said to bear the mark of its maker," answered the warrior. "I do not recall the marking of the first Great Evil. Yet, it is said that each rebelling power applies their own. That which I discovered had two rings overlaid. I suspect the Yerch with the darker skin was a new breed from a new master. A new woe set to afflict the world."

"Why not it being one owned by this Prophetess?" said Roe.

Halsedric answered with a shake of his head. "It takes a much greater understanding of dark craft to birth something as vile as a Yerch, and an even greater power to bend them to the will of their maker. She had no such power. While she was quite learned in dark lore, her greatest weapon was cunning and seduction." Then, in a low tone, Halsdric added, "A skill she plied to great effect.

I slew her in a cave—her last refuge it seemed. Yet, she was not alone. Something else was with her there. Hiding in the shadows. Old, deep, and malevolent. The runes etched into the steel of my sword gleamed white hot in the encompassing flame. A sign I know now was a warning. That one of the devils of that elder age was there."

"Did you slay it?"

"No," Halsedric answered. "I had not the understanding that I have now. I was badly maimed. And now, as I recall that moment, I fear there was little I could do."

"Why?" said Roe.

"My blade, while a mighty weapon, may only destroy that which is bound to this world," answered Halsedric.

Roe's brow furrowed. "Cannot destroy spirit? What can?"

"The Allfather, I suspect," Halsedric said with a shrug of his shoulders.

Roe went oddly quiet. Then the trapper's expression turned confused, if not angry.

"What troubles you?" said Halsedric.

"I don't mean to speak ill of the Allfather, but that don't make much sense. I mean, if'n the Allfather has undone one of them devils in the past, why not all of them? Why must we be troubled by them?"

His head turned to one side, Halsedric considered Roe's question for a moment. "It is not my place to say. My purpose in the world is to bring an end to these aberrations as they are found. And for that purpose, my dead flesh was reclaimed and thus anointed. It is why I wield this mighty sword."

"Aye, but, if'n you cannot undo spirit—"

"Roe," Halsedric interjected, "we are a fallen people. As a consequence, we are afflicted by evil until the time of the end. The wise may argue and debate as to a greater meaning of this burden we must bear and the afflictions we must suffer. Yet, what is certain is that while redemption may be freely given to those who hold fast to belief and faith, the path that must be traveled is long and beset with many perils. One may question it. Some may rage against it. In the end, the path still remains.

As to why such things exist to trouble us? Are we not a burden unto ourselves? Do we not quarrel? Do we not conspire, steal, and slay one another? One cannot rage against the Allfather and claim injury when we have ourselves injured others without cause."

Roe went to argue, but Halsedric interrupted him again. "As to why the Allfather does not simply wish away the existence of such sufferings, I might offer some wisdom. We are naught but dust and mud, given life by the breath from the Creator's own lips. We are sons of a sort, having a part of Him within us all. The very spark that defines our being came from Him. As any father loves his son, so the Allfather loves all His creations. Trees. Grass. Friend and family. He too made them, as He made the Host of the West. Would you ask Him to unmake us so readily for the evils we have done?"

Head bowed, Roe muttered low, "Well…no."

"Perhaps this, then, is the reason why those things we deem as evil are left to linger," said Halsedric.

After a moment's pause Roe looked up and shook his head. "Yet, you don't know for certain? Don't the Herald answer these questions?"

"I do not ask these questions," replied Halsedric. "It is not my place to do so."

"But don't you ever wonder?"

"Yes. There are times I ponder such things," Halsedric replied. "Yet, when one has been in the presence of a Messenger of the Allfather, one does not linger long on questions for which there is no answer. No answer other than to have faith that what is revealed to you is all you need know. Not only do I linger in the light, but I must, at times, gaze into the Abyss. When one has seen both, one does not question overlong things that are far from their understanding. For in each, there is both glory and terror."

While there was a sort of ambivalence in his expression before, Halsedric's face turned suddenly stern, those pale eyes having a stare both serious and cold. And when he spoke, his words were deliberate, mournful, and ominous. "Yet as one who has seen both, I will say to you this—I would rather remain in the light. For what dwells there in the darkness simmers in madness and malice."

As quickly as Halsedric's expression changed, it became placid once more as he asked, "Does this satisfy your curiosity?"

Eyes down, Roe nodded his head sheepishly.

Seeing this, Halsedric spoke once again. "Do not feel shame in questioning such things. It was through understanding that you came to your belief. Yet, there are times when one must simply do as one is told."

Not long after, Herodiani strolled into the barn casually, a chunk of bread in her hand.

Seeing the huntress arrive, Roe turned his attention to her as he spoke. "So, we're travelin' at night."

Herodiani nodded, opening her mouth to eat the small piece she pulled from the loaf, only to halt as Halsedric spoke.

"And our friends?"

"All is calm," she answered.

"Friends?" said Roe, his gaze alternating between the huntress and Halsedric. "What friends?"

"After we were attacked on that first night, I called for aid," answered Halsedric. "Six Elanni soldiers patrol the lands around this farm."

"I ain't seen no soldiers," said Roe.

"And you may never see them," said Herodiani.

"How?" said Roe, befuddled.

"How?" repeated the huntress, unsure of the question being asked.

"How'd you call them? Your friends?"

"You saw a bird the colors of blue and amber, yes?" responded Halsedric.

"Aye," nodded Roe.

"It is a Kingslark," continued Halsedric. "Used since ancient days as messengers by the Ageless."

"How's that work then?" said Roe, looking a little perplexed. The brow beneath his dark mop of hair creased as those narrow eyes turned deeply curious.

Before the question could be answered, Herodiani interrupted the conversation. Using the piece of bread that she held in her fingers, she pointed to both Roe and Halsedric saying, "If we are to travel at night, you two should sleep. That you might be rested for the journey."

Roe stammered, "But—"

"Herodiani speaks truth," added Halsedric. "Sleep now. We can discuss this further at a later time." After he spoke, he turned to his things and began to dig around.

As Roe made his bed ready, he saw Halsedric pull from his gear the note he secreted away from the villa of Lord Karne. As Halsedric unfolded the paper, Roe spoke up. "Ain't you going to sleep?"

As Halsedric analyzed the symbols on the paper, he answered, "Soon. I wish to try my hand at revealing what is hidden here in these markings." Looking up, he called out to

Herodiani, “Bring me that quill and ink you brought with you.”

CHAPTER FOURTEEN

NOT ONLY WAS TRAVEL BY NIGHT DIFFICULT FOR Roe, the trio was moving along paths that were far different than he was accustomed to. They stayed away from the roads and avoided the villages, moving along the fences of homesteads, and finding shelter in the scattered clusters of trees that dotted the open landscape. Traveling outside his normal routes, Roe had difficulty gauging the landmarks. Yet, fearful that the various associates of Karne and the mysterious cloaked devotees might await them along the trail, less predictable paths were taken. So now, they had only the stars and the position of the moon to direct their path, as well as the rising and setting sun.

The further east they traveled, the more sparse the population became. Hedgerows that divided crowded plots were a rare sighting. Tilled fields and the sounds of herding sheep grew less frequent the further they wandered away from Farmer Hale's lands. Wild grasses and low shrubs grew unfettered. Lowland moors, filled with sedges and reeds, impeded their progress, as did large outcrops and ledges of brown stone. Abandoned farms dotted the landscape along their passage. Fields of grain mixed with grasses grew in disorderly arrangements and delineating hedgerows grew untamed. Houses of sod and stone were left empty, unmaintained shelters collapsed, pens abandoned, and weeds were left unchecked by grazing animals and allowed to grow wild.

Their first night was spent in such a place, the evening passing uneventfully. The only controversy to be had was the baying of a lone wolf somewhere in the distance out on the friendless grasslands. A sound that would prompt Roe to comment, "You'll hear less of that the further east we go."

On the morning next, a lone figure was spotted on the distant horizon as they paused atop a high knoll. The sighting was almost coincidental, Herodiani and her keen Elanni eyes detecting a dark form disappearing behind a hill. Such wariness on the move was a common practice when journeying in the wilds where bandits, and worse, were known to frequent.

They continued their trek for a time, changing direction to see if they were being followed. After an hour or so, they halted their journey, finding a suitable hill by which the land around them could be surveyed. Thereafter, Herodiani flipped up the hood of her cloak before dismounting.

Roe, Halsedric, and the horses slipped behind the crest of the hill, where they could remain unseen. There, they waited as the huntress surveyed the land around them, hidden by the magic of her cloak.

"You sure there was somethin' out there?" questioned Roe of Halsedric as the pair waited atop their mounts. "I ain't seen no one followin' us."

"The eyes of the Elanni are keener than that of men. If she saw something, you can be assured it was there."

"Just one? One ain't much of a threat to us."

One of the horses snorted as Halsedric asked, "How many do you know travel these lands alone?"

"Well, I don't rightfully know," answered Roe as he shrugged his shoulders. "I take a route closer to the river. But, I'm supposin' not many. What might you be gettin' at?"

With a quick glance up the hill, Halsedric replied, "There are few who wander the wilds alone. Those who know not the peril that may befall them in such places. Those who have no choice but to travel unaccompanied. And then there are those who have naught to fear when they travel the trail alone. They have no fear, for they are the peril that dwells in the wilderness."

"But it's only one man," countered Roe. "I've seen you take a blade to the gut and nary bat an eye. What man's goin' to fell you?"

Halsedric turned his head and addressed Roe. "As one who stalks game in the wilds, you, of all men, should be most aware of the benefits of stealth."

Looking a little ashamed for not thinking that, it took Roe a moment before he spoke again. "So, if'n it's trouble that's followin' us, how do you think he'll come at us?"

Halsedric thought on the question for a moment before answering. "He will follow our trail until we encamp, then wait from afar until sleep finds us. Then, using the dark as a cloak, he will strike."

"Well, it ain't hard to track us across the grass," offered Roe. "I'd take us over some stone were there any about. If'n we find a stream, we might lose him, were there one near. Then we could double back, and—"

Just then, Herodiani appeared, pulling back the hood of her cloak. Roe nearly leapt from his saddle from fright. The horse he rode stomped its hooves and grumbled discontentedly as Roe muttered a curse softly beneath his breath.

Halsedric and the Lenogala, however, were unfazed by the sudden appearance of the huntress. “What did you discover?” Halsedric asked of Herodiani, his eyes fixed on her with a keen interest.

“A single traveler,” said Herodiani with confidence. “Downwind and mounted. Taking great pains to follow our trail and remain hidden from view.”

After gathering his wits once more, Roe said, “Mayhaps we can double back, like I—”

“And chance we lose our pursuer?” interrupted Halsedric. He shook his head and added, “No. I will not risk another of our hosts. Rather we draw the hunter to us, on the ground of our choosing.”

Roe scanned the terrain around him in the sudden lull of the debate. Turning his head north, he paused for a moment before turning back to Halsedric. “Mayhaps we continue east for a spell, then head north for the remainder of the day. Find us an empty ‘stead to make camp, like we did evenin’ last. Sound like what you was lookin’ for?”

Both the warrior and the huntress considered this in silence. As they did, a fluttering of feathered wings and sharp chirps announced the arrival of the blue bird with the orange crest. Wings splayed and talons out, the passerine creature landed deftly on the shoulder of the huntress, turning its head and chirping a second time. Herodiani seemed oblivious to the creature’s existence as its slim digits gripped the moss green cloth of her cloak.

"It is as sound a plan as any," said Halsedric.

"Agreed," added Herodiani.

His horse moved forward before turning to face Roe. Nodding his head at Roe, Halsedric said, "Very well. Lead on."

They spent at least two hours maintaining their eastward trek before they struck north, continuing in that direction for the remainder of the day. Along this new route, they followed a high ridge, passing along lands that were occupied and tended, farms clustered together in a community of sorts. It was, perhaps, one of the last they saw during their passage that day. As the afternoon dragged on, they came across another vacated homestead. A primitive estate near a small stream that consisted of a cluster of buildings whose walls were formed of sod and mud and whose thatched roofs were in an advanced state of disrepair. Grass grew knee-high, with no one and nothing there to trample it down.

The walls of the house were still sound, though little else was. Encroaching water was rotting the timber trusses of the roof. The leather straps that acted as hinges for the door had rotted away. The shutters of the windows were missing, as was the wood of the door, no doubt scavenged by local passersby for firewood in prior years. The inside was utterly empty, devoid of any trappings that might have shown prior occupation. The dirt floor of the abode was still damp at one end, the rain from a recent storm having made its way through the failing roof.

"This will do," said Halsedric.

As they were unloading their mounts, Roe asked, "So, what's next?"

After he slung a set of loaded bags over his shoulder from his Lenogala steed, Halsedric turned and surveyed the land around them. Pointing to a distant structure near where they approached the abandoned farm, Halsedric replied, "Herodiani will maintain a hidden watch there, bow at the ready." Turning back, he looked at Roe, adding, "You will shelter in the main house near the doorway. Take a place near the wall and build a fire in the hearth."

"What? Won't that let the whole world know where we are?"

"Indeed," said Halsedric with a confident stare. "If our pursuer has any skill, he will scout the outbuildings first."

Turning to the eastern end of the house, Halsedric continued. "We will quarter the horses on that end and conceal my presence among them. It should be dark enough that our pursuer will not be able to see a yard line or hobbles on the mounts. Either way, he will avoid them, lest the beasts sense him and raise an alarm. His focus will be on the main house and the light within."

Pointing to the doorway, Halsedric continued. "There is but one way in and out. He will hold fast to the wall and peek in through the window." Turning to Herodiani, he motioned off in the distance, away from the domicile, saying, "You will remain hidden in the dark. As he nears the door, use your bow."

"Slay him?" said the huntress.

"No," Halsedric replied, lowering his arm. "Wound him in the leg. I would rather take him captive than slay him. Then, we can release him into the custody of our allies."

"You want to capture him, just to take him to Gallain's 'stead?" remarked Roe, puzzled. "I thought the whole point was to keep him away from them folk?"

"I would rather interrogate him before delivering him to the Elanni," replied Halsedric.

"Whatever you say," grumbled Roe. He stuffed some of his gear beneath his arm before disappearing past the threshold of the abandoned house.

Eventually, darkness descended, the night's sky troubled by broken clouds above. Despite it not being a full moon, it still shone brightly. The night creatures sang their songs, the scattered clicking and chirping of insects among the green grasses accompanying the gentle whisper of the breeze when it blew. While the heat of the day had lessened, the wind still blew warm in the evenings. Halsedric sat on the ground, legs out, his back against the hardened mud that formed the wall of the home. Much of the sky was hidden by the wide eaves, though he could stare out past them to marvel at the swirl of stars that ornamented the heavens. One of the Lenogala snorted, and another shook its head as it rested with him in the grasses.

His sword lay next to him on the ground, in ready reach of his hand. He had hoped that he wouldn't need to draw his blade, for the vengeance contained within the blessed steel was for those things beyond that of petty mortals and scheming men. Silently, he prayed, petitioning the Allfather for guidance. Lifting himself slightly, he looked past the house, wondering if he could see Herodiani hiding in the open. The darkness and the magic of her cloak made that impossible. If he couldn't see her, neither could their unwelcomed guest, or so he reasoned.

Bored, he pulled free a thin stem of a grass shoot and stuck it between his teeth. It was these small slices of solitudinous introspection that prompted him to recall some of the fonder moments of his early years. Those precious moments in his youth where he could steal away to hide beneath the stout boughs of a mighty oak, dreaming away the remainder of the day. Life was much simpler back then. Tutors and chores. Brothers and sisters with whom he could pester and plot. The thrill of catching a fish on a hook and playing at war with sticks as swords.

Lost in his thoughts and remembrances, he had barely noticed the sudden lull in the night sounds. It was a snort from one of the Lenogala that caught his attention, the horse alerting him that someone was approaching.

He plucked his blade from the ground and lifted to his knees. The horses remained silent, even those of Roe doing their part to help trap the stranger in their midst. Peering past the horse next to him, he turned his head to let his peripheral vision aid him in the dark.

At first, all he saw was darkness, though forms hazy and indistinct were perceived. Then, he saw something move in and around some of the detached structures of the abandoned farm. A dark mass that darted from building to building as it scouted the surrounding area. Halsedric would lose this moving glob of black, blocked by the walls of the house.

His hand gripped the sheath of his sword as he waited, his ears straining to hear the snap of a bow string and the soft whistle of an arrow cut the air. As the seconds seemed to stretch into long hours, Halsedric's anticipation grew almost to a fevered pitch. Eyes closed, he turned his ear in Herodiani's direction and listened intently, letting the rest of the world fade away.

Then, the trap was sprung. An arrow hissed in the night, and there was a sharp grunt as it found its mark.

"Scatter," Halsedric whispered to the horses. On command, those beasts that lay with him on the ground rose swiftly. The whole of them turned and dispersed, moving away from the house and spreading out in the yard. Another missile flew, and there was a loud yelp as Herodiani hit the mysterious stranger again. Halsedric lifted to his feet. Quickly, he stepped away from the house and drew his blade, lest he set the house ablaze. Satisfied when the blade did not catch fire, he rounded the corner of the main home.

There was a commotion in the house as Roe rose to his feet. A low fire in the crude hearth cast an orange light that spilled out from the doorway and the windows. Despite that, it did little to illuminate the exterior of the house. Luckily, Roe had been wise enough to have lit his lamp and have it at the ready. When Roe lifted the device, the sundown orange from the fire merged with the stronger amber glow coming from the holes in the brass lamp. It was just enough light to paint the outline of a figure near the entryway of the mud house. Beneath the wide eaves, their mysterious pursuer knelt, two white-fletched arrows poking out from the dark fabric that covered him. One, it seemed, had struck the meaty portion of his thigh. A second landed further back, appearing to have embedded itself deep in the stranger's posterior. Yet, the one thing that caught Halsedric's eye was the short sharp sword held in the hand of the wounded man.

Shifting his sword to his other hand, Halsedric stepped forward slowly and stuck his arm through the small window, saying, "Roe, lend me the lamp."

The stranger stood, though he was unsteady on his feet. His head lifted as he stuck out his blade in warning, letting all know that he was still dangerous, even when wounded.

His fingers feeling the brass ring on the top of the lamp, Halsedric pulled the light through the window and let the glow of the lamp fall upon the stranger in their midst. Like those who tried to abduct Halsedric at the Hale farm, this stranger was also clad in black. A similarly-hued cloth covered the man's face, save for the eyes, which glared menacingly at the warrior.

The man shuffled back, letting slip a pinched growl as his eyes closed tightly due to the pain. It was clear to the warrior that their pursuer was going nowhere quickly.

Soon, Herodiani approached, sword and dagger drawn. She positioned herself in a manner where she might intercept the mysterious man should he attempt to retreat from Halsedric. The man's head turned back and around, taking note of the approach of the Elanni maiden. He did not look to her overlong. His vengeful stare soon fixed on Halsedric.

"Yield," Halsedric said to the would-be assassin as he lifted the lamp and took one small step forward. The man in black shuffled back in reply, growling in pain.

"Lay down your weapons, and your life will be spared. We have no desire to slay you, yet if you persist—"

Halsedric's requests were cut short as the man turned the blade about in his hands. Then, with a singular swift thrust, he impaled himself on his own blade.

"No!" Halsedric cried out as he vainly lunged forward. Despite his quick reflexes, the act of the mysterious assassin was too unexpected, and Halsedric was too far away to stop him.

The man in black fell to his knees, then—as if on purpose—he fell forward on the blade, the weapon penetrating deeper into his abdomen. A shaft of one of Herodiani's arrows snapped as the man rolled over on his side, mortally wounded.

CHAPTER FIFTEEN

"ARROCK HARASATHUR. ARRAOCK MELOSOTHUR. Harrock bathu, bathu, romosatha!"

The man in black whispered the chant over and over again as he lay there on the dirt floor of the house. His self-inflicted wound was fatal, despite their attempts to staunch the bleeding. The blade cut too deeply. Too much damage was done. All they could do was wait until he passed from consciousness to the slumber that heralds oblivion. They cut away the cloth from around his face and head. Once ruddy and filled with life, the man's skin was turning pale. The dark eyes that glared malevolently at Halsedric only minutes before stared at the roof, glassy and seemingly disconnected from reality.

Halsedric, Roe, and Herodiani sat on the ground, dispersed around the empty space of the interior. Their backs resting against the cool dirt wall, they stared at the man as he chanted those mysterious words in his final moments.

"What you think he's sayin'?" asked Roe. His question received no reply.

Halsedric quietly suspected they were somehow tied to the strange runes and script he had discovered in recent years.

"I don't think your prayers of healin' is goin' to work this time," Roe continued, tired of the silence.

"It is for the Allfather to decide," countered Halsedric, his mind preoccupied with other matters.

The chanting went on for an hour or more, the voice of the stranger growing weaker as time wore on. The words were spoken with a singular focus, the stranger barely acknowledging the party, and refusing water when offered. Then his voice went silent. Steady breathing turned ragged and shallow. Less than an hour before dawn, he ceased to breathe altogether.

By that time, Herodiani had departed, finding a spot outside to keep watch for more potential surprises. Roe slept while Halsedric remained awake, contemplating the events of that evening. They had at least another day's worth of travel, and he needed rest. Yet something preoccupied his mind and his senses. What it was, he did not know.

Having drifted off to sleep momentarily, Halsedric awoke when morning was upon them. Roe was still dozing, curled up on the ground near the doorway. Only a few glowing embers remained in the hearth, a crude opening fixed into the far wall made of clay brick and mud. Outside, somewhere in the distance, a bird sang a song to welcome the sun, offering a measure of hope for the new day.

Rising, Halsedric made his way to the body of the stranger and searched the remains. Almost immediately, he came upon another medallion hidden beneath his clothes. With two of these already in his possession, he left it remaining about the man's neck. Not long after this discovery, Halsedric discovered markings on the man's pale skin. Inked lettering that started from the line of each shoulder, forming a semi-circle along the man's chest. This was something new. He had not seen these on the other men who were slain at the home of Farmer Hale.

His inspection was interrupted by Herodiani, who entered into the room. "I have found the man's horse. What are your thoughts on what we should do with our pursuer?" Her voice roused Roe, who groaned sleepily as he raised his head from the pack he used as a pillow.

Halsedric stared at the dead man for a time in silence. Part of him wanted to leave the body at the site, hidden somewhere among the wreckage of the homestead. Yet, there was something in him that felt the need to bring the body with them. He debated for a time in silence before Herodiani said, "Halsedric?"

"Let us wrap him in a blanket and lash him to his mount. We will bury his remains near the home of Farmer Gallain. How much further need we travel?"

Still lying on the ground, one eye closed and his chin resting on his pack, Roe replied, "Another day of travel if'n we didn't have to travel north. Mayhaps a day and a half, if'n we ride hard, but I'm supposin' two."

"Very well," answered Halsedric with a yawn. "Let us eat, clear our tracks, and be off."

After they ate, Halsedric searched through the nameless man's effects while Roe cleaned the site. He found very little in the way of identification. There was a small pouch of gold coins, a bow with a small number of arrows, several daggers, and a cache of several vials. These Halsedric opened and smelled, immediately detecting poison. It confirmed all the warrior needed to know. He didn't know whether they had been stalked since they left the Hale homestead, or if their paths crossed as a matter of coincidence. Yet had it not been for the keen eyes of the Elanni maiden, one or more of them may have exchanged places with the dead assassin.

It would be another two hours before they were on their way east. Halsedric held the reins of the assassin's horse and guided it as they rode. Roe guided them in a southerly direction, with an eastward bent.

While this leg of the journey was far less eventful than the prior day, Halsedric could not shake the feeling that something was amiss. He couldn't lay a finger as to what it was that bothered him. As the day dragged on, the feeling of unease grew stronger. He noticed how the other mounts avoided the corpse. Even the one that bore the body of the dead man became difficult to manage.

As the night neared, they made camp near a rise of brown stone in a shallow depression between two hills. As the others went about unburdening the beasts, Halsedric unlashed the dead body from the horse. Roe, watching from afar, made a remark that echoed what Halsedric was already thinking as he lifted the dead assassin off the horse. "That body be mighty limber bein' dead that long. Should be stiff by now."

Once removed, the horse trotted away, the Lenogala moving to corral the anxious horse. As Halsedric laid the corpse on the grass-strewn ground, Herodiani drew near. In her native tongue she said, "The horses sense something amiss. They do not like the smell of the body."

"I must confess, I have been greatly vexed since he died," he said of the slain assassin. "Something here is amiss, yet I know naught from whence it comes."

"Perhaps dark sorceries are at work?"

Halsedric did not answer her. Instead, he turned to Roe, who was setting his saddle on the ground. "Find me two thongs, if you would."

"What do you intend to do?" said Herodiani.

His brow furrowed, Halsedric looked down at the body wrapped and bound in the dead man's own blanket. "I am going to bind his hands and feet."

"To what end?"

Down Halsedric went, kneeling at the corpse. He unbound the rope that lashed the blanket about the body and unrolled the bundle, leaving the dead man's corpse face down in the grass. Roe approached, two long lengths of leather dangling from his fingers. Halsedric took one and set about pulling back the hands of the corpse, binding them together behind the assassin's back.

"Bind his feet," Halsedric commanded Roe.

"What?" said Roe, befuddled by the request.

Halsedric paused to look up at Roe. "Bind his feet."

"The man's dead." Roe's voice was exasperated as well as confused. "He ain't goin' nowhere."

"If you will not—"

"If'n that's what you want, I'll do it," answered Roe, resigned. Soon after, he knelt on the ground and crossed the dead man's feet together before binding them securely. Once done, he rose and wiped his hands on his vest. "What else you lookin' to do?"

"That is all," answered Halsedric as he started to wrap the body once more.

After darkness descended, Roe used some cakes of dried dung along with pieces of the rotted timber he salvaged from the prior camp and made a small fire. Soon after, Herodiani departed to make her patrols for the night. The dim light of the fire cast shadows in the nooks and crannies of the broken brown stone of the hillside where they made their camp.

Roe pulled out his pipe and started to smoke, partly to pass the time, and partly to scent the air with something other than burning dung. Halsedric, on the other hand, sat up, alert, his eyes fixed on the dead body of the assassin across the fire. Next to him sat the assassin's blade and his own. A familiar and terrible sensation ran the length of his spine, that cold chill he felt whenever evil was near.

A horse snorted in the distance, then another as the beasts strayed far from the camp. Halsedric noticed this, though he had no desire to ask one of the Lenogala horses why they feared to stray too near. He already knew the answer to that question.

The body on the other side of the fire twitched. It was subtle. Roe was oblivious, his head down as he softly hummed a tune and puffed on the stem of his pipe. Halsedric, however, watched with intense interest. Those pale eyes of his were fixed on the covered body of the assassin, the warrior almost wishing it would move again. Anything to validate the unease that troubled him since they left that abandoned farm.

Soon, the body twitched again. The blanket that covered the body sighed and shook as the motion of the corpse continued, even to the point where Roe noticed.

Stunned by the sudden animation of something that was long dead, the pipe fell from the trapper's mouth, the smoldering ash and cinders of the burning weed falling into his lap. The trapper squeaked as he jumped, panicked, batting away the burning orange flecks from his groin and legs.

Halsedric took no time in rising to his feet, grabbing the short blade of the assassin, and rounding the fire. By now, the formerly lifeless mass of the dead man twitched and twisted. From beneath the covers of the blanket, a muffled voice could be heard. It was croaking and cracked, uttering something that sounded like words, though far fouler. The warrior paused at the body, bending over to pull back the flaps of the blanket.

The assassin's body continued to squirm as Halsedric grabbed the upper left arm and turned the animated corpse face up. As it did, the growling utterances continued. Its opaque milky eyes were open and staring back at him. The flesh was still pale and cold, the lips a deathly shade of blue as they moved and twisted.

Roe spoke in an astounded whisper. "What in the—"

"One final snare for us to trip," answered Halsedric as he stared down menacingly at the body.

"How'd you know?"

"I did not know," replied Halsedric, continuing to glare down at the writhing corpse. "When one wrestles with devils and the damned, one learns there is wisdom in an abundance of caution."

As the face of the creature twisted, it snarled something indistinct, the sounds it uttered seeming more like a curse. Halsedric dropped to his knees. Taking the assassin's short sword in hand, he lifted the blade into the air. With a single, furious stroke that cleaved flesh and bone, he cut off the head of the animated abomination.

The night thereafter was silent as any other, though the disquiet of the events plagued Roe in his sleep, the trapper turning and mumbling as he slept.

Near noon the next day, they finally came to the homestead of Farmer Gallain, a lonely patch of land that was well tended by the farmer, his sons, and his daughters. Smaller than the parcel of land owned by Farmer Hale, it was also more diversified, having more and varied livestock. There were also fewer and smaller dwellings, and only a single granary made of stone and roofed with thatch.

By the time they reached their destination, they were saddle-sore, hungry, and tired. Gallain, the patriarch, had a long face, the years of toil tending the land having left its mark in his flesh. His cheeks drooped and the heavy bags beneath his eyes caused his lids to sag. His crown was a mop of gray and black hair that was cut roughly above his shoulders, no doubt tended to by his wife with a knife or woolen shears. His gait was a lumbering one, the remnants of his hard physique still apparent, though age and time had taken some of his quickness and vigor. All in all, he struck Halsedric as a friendly sort, having a smile on his lips as Roe hailed him. Thereafter, the farmer called to one of his sons, whom he dispatched to summon a neighbor to meet with his guests.

The smile faded, however, when the farmer saw the corpse lashed to the horse Halsedric led by the reins. He also seemed to age further as Roe briefly explained to Gallain the troubling details of their trip.

CHAPTER SIXTEEN

STEPPING ACROSS THE THRESHOLD, A BOWL IN each hand, the farmer named Gallain stooped to avoid hitting his head on the beam above. It was a common habit of his, even though he could clear the opening with an inch or two to spare. For all his life, well over forty years, he had gone in and out of that doorway more times than he could count. It only took a few times in his awkward youth to learn the painful reminder that he was far taller than the ancestors who had raised the structure many generations past.

Lifting the bowls into the air, Gallain's lips now expressed a true grin. "It may not look like much, but the wife makes a fine stew. There'll be sopbread soon if'n you wants some."

Down went the bowl in front of Halsedric, the bottom of it gliding against the stained and worn wood of the table, the grain of the top reflecting long years of constant use. Made of thick pine timbers and preserved with wax, its amber color was now more of a muddied brown, the knots of wood nearly hidden with endless use.

Roe had been standing at the far side of the interior, foot upon a slate hearth, chatting with a neighboring farmer named Old Sam. Old Sam was perfectly content squatting on his stool, puffing on the long and gracefully curved stem of his pipe as Roe asked his questions in a low voice.

A curious-looking fellow, Old Sam was a slip of a man, long past tending the land himself. He was more content with letting his sons care for the daily chores of the farm. Thick white hairs curled around his chin and jaws, his bald crown glorified by a garland of snowy curls that was wild and untamed like the bleached wool of a sheared sheep.

Both men dressed very much in the manner of Farmer Hale and his sons. Curiously, the clothes they wore seemed not so worn. Their linen shirts, while sporting the ghosts of stains in their weave, were mostly white and clean. Their hands were washed and the dirt scraped from their nails. The woolen vests looked well maintained, and their trousers thick and absent patches. Whether Gallain and his friend had prepared for their visit or if this was their normal state of dress was unclear. Still, Halsedric found it unusual that the weave and the cut of their garments were as refined as they were, being as remote as this homestead was.

When his bowl thumped on the table, Roe's head turned with a snap. Quietly excusing himself from his conversation, he strode quickly over to the table, a carven stool waiting for him. It took him no time to pull the bowl close and start in on the meal.

While Roe ate like a ravenous beast, Halsedric was more restrained in his mannerisms. The warrior blew on the steaming concoction from the earthen bowl before consuming it. Surprised, he hummed his delight as he chewed, no longer hesitant for another bite.

The grin on Gallain's face grew wider as he gauged Halsedric's reaction. From behind him, propped against the stone wall, he took a chair and made his seat at the head of the table. "Good, eh?"

Halsedric nodded as another spoonful went into his mouth. Roe, however, barely looked up from his bowl, consuming the fare with abandon.

"A fine cook, my wife," Gallain continued, his hand motioning to Halsedric's bowl.

One of Gallain's daughters entered, something cradled in her upturned apron. It was a brown loaf not much larger than the bowls provided for the stew, and just as tall. Their host pivoted in his chair, the wood of the back creaking against his weight, and the feet of it scraping the wooded clapboards beneath their feet. “Thank’ee,” he said as he lifted the loaf from her possession. Setting the bread on the table between Halsedric and Roe, he motioned to the loaf, silently offering it to his guests.

Roe took no time to stand on ceremony or manners. He crudely tore the loaf in half, claiming his portion and leaving the remainder for Halsedric. The sound reminded Halsedric of the cutting of a burlap bag, having the crisp sound of split fibers and the low reverberating thump of footsteps on wood. His bowl half empty now, Halsedric took up the remainder of the bread and inspected it briefly.

The dark brown loaf was often called Horsebread by the denizens of the cities. Though here in the open lands and fields of simpler folk, it was the staple of their diet. Partly made of wheat, stale beer, roughly ground peas, and millet, it was leavened with a sour starter that only a good wife would possess and fastidiously maintain. This was not the airy loaf of nobles and kings, but dense and hearty for those who needed the nourishment to get them through each day. Halsedric tore off a piece and dipped it into the stew, pulling up a lump all bready and brown before stuffing it into his mouth.

Hearing the scrape of a stool against the floor, Halsedric turned his head quickly to note the company of Old Sam at the table before returning his attention to his host.

"You fancy folk ain't probably used to such," noted Gallain.

Shaking his head to the contrary, Halsedric took his time answering, chewing, and swallowing before his reply. "Fine food, good sir."

Seemingly satisfied, Gallain leaned back in his chair, his face beaming with pride. "We ain't used to travelers out here. 'Tis good to see a friendly face now and again."

Pulling off another chunk, Halsedric went about lazily dipping it into his stew. "It is good to be received in such a gracious manner. My compliments to your bride. She is a fine cook."

"Aye, that she is," remarked Old Sam with a nod, pulling the stem of the pipe from his mouth. Sweet-smelling smoke wafted out from his lips as he spoke. His voice was high, thin, and haggard as was typical of a man of his advanced years. Still, you could hear the forcefulness of it behind the layers of age. A tough man who was used to barking his orders at equally tough sons.

The broad smile faded from Gallain's face as his head fell. "A troubling tale you tell of your journey here, though it don't surprise me none," Gallain said. His eyes shifted their gaze between Halsedric and Roe as he added, "Been hearin' some strange goin's on down in the south."

As Halsedric chewed, the farmer pulled his chair forward and rested his arms on the table. He went to speak, but stopped, noticing Roe's empty bowl. "Another?"

A nod and a grunt was Roe's answer, his mouth too full to do otherwise.

Leaning back slightly, the farmer called out, "Sadie! More stew."

As Gallain relaxed in his chair, his daughter entered swiftly, wiping her hands on her apron. Approaching the corner of the table, she leaned over and took the empty bowl, departing quickly.

"The lands hereabout be peaceable for the most," said Gallain. "We're far out from the city and its troubles. Ain't much happening 'round here, save for the fox, or a wolf or two looking to filch a quick meal from some herdsman's flocks.

"Weren't always that way," Old Sam interjected.

"Raiders?" Halsedric said, looking briefly at Farmer Gallain.

"Aye," Gallain answered, drumming his fingers on the top of the table. "We ain't seen much of them these days. Mostly strange folk keeping to the far fringes of our lands."

"To what destination?" said Halsedric.

Sam grumbled, "The Wychwood, I suppose. Spring and autumn without fail."

As Sadie returned with a full bowl for Roe, Halsedric took another piece of bread and scooped up a helping of the steaming stew. "Tell me more of the Wychwood," he said as he popped the bread into his mouth and began to chew.

Halsedric nodded responsively as Sam began to speak. "Bad place. Cursed, some say. Shunned by all who tend the land. Been like that ere I was born. These lands was once owned by the House of Aelbrech, given as a gift to those who fought in the war."

"The War of the Prophets," said Halsedric, finishing Sam's sentence as he took another mouthful of food.

"Aye, that. And the one to unseat King—" Gallain stalled, his head turning to one side as his mind feverishly raced to remember the name. Leaning back in his seat, he grumbled to himself, "What was his name?"

"Castor," piped up Sam. "Called him Castor the Cruel, if'n I recollect."

"Right," Gallain answered as he leaned forward again. "Castor the Cruel, he was. Follower of some witch in the north. Said she showed him visions and whatnot." The farmer chuckled softly to himself for a moment before continuing. "Since then, the city and the lands hereabout been ruled by a council of nobles, though they don't bother us much out here. Most of us who live out this way had forefathers that fought in that war. They was given lands closer to the wood, though most of 'em moved on long ago. Lived *too* close to the wood, if'n you ask me."

"Yes," answered Halsedric after swallowing. "So, I have been told. What is it that makes this place cursed? What stories have you heard?"

"Been lots of stories told `bout that place, though I don't recall them at the moment," answered Gallain.

"I gots one," Sam said quickly.

"You mean Ol' Graypa?" Gallain said with a turn of his head. His tone was dubious and his gaze doubtful as he directed his attentions to the elder of the pair.

"Aye," answered Sam with a nod. The stem of his pipe wedged into the corner of his mouth, he hunched forward. With another plume of smoke exiting his lips, he sat up straight and plucked the pipe from his mouth. After an examination of the ash in his bowl he added, "Never known him to lie."

All eyes shifted to Sam as he pulled himself closer to the table. His gaze, however, was on his pipe as he fidgeted with the thing. "Quiet man, he was, my Ol' Graypa."

Sam paused playing with his pipe for a moment as he seemingly contemplated something in the back of his mind. "His hair was as white as mountain snows. My Pa once told me that his hair had been white since he was a young'un. But it weren't always so. Never thought much of it until one night, when Ol' Graypa told me the story `bout how that came to be."

Sam looked up at the others with keen eyes whose character bordered on mischievous. A master storyteller in his own right, Sam seemed to draw them all in as he continued his tale. "Graypa and I was sittin' in front of the fire. He had been drinkin' that night, like he was oft to do. Pa said my Graypa had been takin' to the drop more and more the older he got."

"I remember I was whittlin' on a stick when Graypa told me his tale, `bout when he was a young lad himself. Bold and brash. A real handful even by his own reckonin'."

"Well, it seems his sister got bit by a viper one day. His Pa set off to one of the homesteads in the south to find somethin' or someone to help. My Graypa, bein' the headstrong one he was, stole a horse and made off to the wood."

"Why the Wychwood?" said Halsedric, his brow furrowed as he chewed his bread and stew.

"Aye," Sam answered with a nod. "Been believed 'round these parts there is a weed that grows there, said to cure any poison."

"Torin's Wort," interjected Gallain.

Sam nodded and used the curved stem of his pipe to point at the farmer. "That be the one."

Sam continued, "Rode day and night he did, near killin' the beast he rode. But he made it to the Wychwood ere eventide the day next. Went deep into them woods lookin' for the weed. Then he said somethin' spooked the horse."

Sam went silent again, but only briefly as his gaze fell. "He didn't say nothin' after, save they found the horse three days later grazin' in a pasture not far from his home. Then they found Ol' Graypa just a-wanderin'—aimless, half-naked. His brown mop turned as white as snow.

"The poison took his sister, his ill-wrought plan all for naught. 'Twas days ere he remembered who and where he be. Whatever he found there in them woods was all but lost somewhere in his head. My Grayma once said Graypa was much changed after he returned from the forest."

With a serious stare and using the stem of his pipe once more to point to the others, he concluded, "Mark my words, there is somethin' in them woods. Somethin' powerful enough to turn my Ol' Graypa's hair white and crack his mind like a pane of glass." Then, as if in defiance, he pushed the stem of his pipe past his lips and clamped down on the tip with his teeth with a subtle click.

"There's more," said Gallain. "It ain't just the Wychwood. Some of them that lived further out claim there is a beast that roams the hills at night. Was said to be ravenous—a scourge that preyed on man and beast alike. I once heard it said it was because of that beast that many up and left their lands and made tracks to the city."

"Has this beast troubled you in the past?" asked Halsedric.

"We ain't had no problems hereabouts," answered the farmer.

Old Sam piped up quickly. "Spent some time with Meyer and his folk few days back. They's closer to the wood than the rest. He's been tellin' of somethin' spookin' his horses. And Felcher's been losin' sheep the last few years. Some to wolves. But some ain't never been found. Only blood and bits of wool and a trail leadin' off east."

"So, the numbers of wolves here has increased as well?" said Halsedric, the two farmers having his rapt attention.

"Aye, wolves have been a plague out here," said Roe, barely looking up from his bowl.

"*Was* a plague," Gallain agreed with a nod. "Weren't too long ago that folk hereabouts were losin' a score of their flock every moon, 'till Roe here come and thinned them wolves out a bit. Wolves always been a problem in these lands. Weren't strange for a shepherd to lose an ewe or two a season. But, it seemed, for a bit, that them beasts were everywhere."

His questioning eyes alternating between the three men, Halsedric asked, "Why the sudden change?"

With half a mouthful of food, Roe answered, "Best I can tell it, the game's been driven west. Where game goes, wolves follow."

"And what is it that drives the game west?" said Halsedric as he scanned the others in the room. There was a long silence that followed, though it was clear everyone knew the answer to the question.

"Ain't just `bout wolves," said Sam. Pointing to Gallain, he added, "Tell 'em `bout the sawyer."

"Aye," Gallain said, eyes closed. "Another local legend."

"Please, continue," said Halsedric, ignoring his stew for the moment.

Gallain leaned back and inhaled deep. His hands fell from the table, rubbing the rough wool of his trousers. "A few generations ago, Lord Aelbrech decided to make profit off the Wychwood. After all, there's a river and a lake that runs its north shore. It ain't much to harvest a few trees and float 'em down the river to the city. Some fine wood can be found there, and sorely needed. Oak. Maple. Ash. Tall ship's-mast pine. None of them wood mills would touch the Wychwood, given the tales goin' `bout. So, Lord Aelbrech hires this sawyer from the north. Paid him a goodly sum of silver, from what I hears.

So, a team wanders to the Wychwood. A moon passes, then another. Naught comes floatin' down the river. Then, a few of their animals start showin' up at the farms, grazing, some still with the yokes on. Since then, naught was heard of that sawyer and his team ever again. And since then, none dare go much further east from here for lumber, or game, or anythin' at all."

Poking and prodding his stew with his spoon, Halsedric spoke after a time. "With all of these troubles, I would assume that a local sheriff or marshal might attend to some of these matters."

"Ain't no sheriff out here," said Gallain, briefly looking at the floor.

"Marshals?" Sam said excitedly. Pursing his lips, the old man turned his head and spat on the ground.

"Sam!" Gallain barked. "You know how the wife feels `bout you doin' that!"

"Apologies," Sam answered, waving his hands about. "But even you know what a useless dung heap them marshals be. 'Specially out here."

Sam's attention turned quickly to Halsedric. Slapping the stem of his pipe back into his mouth with disgust, the old man continued. "Their coin comes from them nobles, and make no mistake, friend, them nobles have some hand in what's goin' on in the wood. Mark my words!"

"It's more than that, Sam," Gallain said as he crossed his arms over his chest. "There's always been talk `bout them lands in and `round the wood. Ruins where ghosts dwell. Ancient tombs of kings buried somewhere in the hills. Old crones that come for young'uns in the night. How else you think the Wychwood got its name?"

As Halsedric finished the last of what was in his bowl, Gallain leaned back in his chair, observing the warrior finish his meal in a moment of silence. Once the last spoonful was consumed, the farmer asked, "So, you've come to cleanse that wood of what ails us? Once and for all?"

His brows raised and head twitching to one side, Halsedric chewed and swallowed before answering. "I seek answers to questions."

It was clear from the look in Gallain's eyes that this was far from a satisfactory answer. "Them woods been a plague in these parts for as long as most can 'member. Most folk hereabout ain't wantin' no trouble. But, if that trouble comes…" The farmer left the statement to dangle, his voice turning suddenly low and silent.

Finished with his bowl, Halsedric let his spoon fall with a muted clack. "You have been very helpful, good sir."

"Well, when you're done here, head round to the missus and take a bowl to that friend you've got out with the horses. The one with the bird on their shoulder. If'n you're headin' out on foot, I'll have a few loaves waitin' for you come morn. Save what portion you've got 'till you hit them trees."

As Roe let out a wet belch, Halsedric nodded and offered a pleasant smile to their host. "You have been more than a gracious host. And I thank you for your hospitality and for the fine meal."

A proud and toothy grin crossed Gallain's face, satisfied with what he had heard. "`Nother bowl? 'Cause if it's to the Wychwood you're going, you'll need all the strength a fine meal can muster."

CHAPTER SEVENTEEN

WHILE THE DAY BROUGHT SUN, THE NIGHT brought rain. There was no fire to pass the darkening of the evening sky. No snapping of wood. No stark, pungent smell of smoke that wafted through the winds. Instead, a fresh scent reminiscent of dew hung heavy in the air, along with the musk of damp hay. The heat of the day had receded, the air now temperate and damp in the dark recesses of Farmer Gallain's barn.

When the day still held sway, the bird with blue and orange plumage sang from the timber rafters above them. Now that night had come, the only sound they heard was the splatter of water as it streamed down from the eaves. Behind them sounded the dense, nasal roar of the droplets as they pummeled the thatch that covered the roof overhead. The world beyond the barn was not only dark, but blurred, the falling rain distorting what little they could see. Their only light was that of the single oil lamp, which Roe had taken from his gear before the storm arrived in earnest.

And somewhere outside, Herodiani was making her rounds, hidden amidst the downpour.

Farmer Gallain braved the early rain, bringing the trio two more loaves of horsebread and some ale, which was greatly appreciated. Halsedric blessed the meal with a prayer before dividing one of the loaves, handing half to Roe, who sat nearby. The second loaf was left untouched and covered with a cloth for the huntress, along with her mug of beer.

But now they had eaten. Their blankets were out and they were sitting on the ground, backs resting against mounded hay. Halsedric used the dim light of the lamp to continue his work on the encoded letter, quill in hand. Flies pestered him and Roe, both insect and man trapped in the interior of that barn. Halsedric, with his uncanny reflexes, was able to bat the pests away with his free hand with little effort.

As for Roe, keeping the flying pests at bay turned into a form of entertainment. The trapper swatted at them when they dared fly too close, often missing. Yet, when he had finally scored a kill, Roe sported a profoundly pleased expression on his face as he flicked the dead fly from his upturned knee. An expression that faded when he discovered Halsedric was unmoved by his little victory. Still, it was something to fill the hours between eating and sleep.

Herodiani eventually arrived, though even with the mysterious powers of her cloak, the rain still revealed her form. The water parted as she passed, coating her hood and the surrounding fabric. As she stepped into the entrance of the barn, she pulled back her hood, the drenching rains sliding off her like water off a duck's down. First resting her bow against the gray fieldstone of the barn's foundation, she unclasped her cloak and removed it. Taking the garment in both hands, she shook it repeatedly to remove what rainwater remained. As the water dripped and collected, a puddle formed at her feet, some of it soaking into the parched hay that littered the ground. Yet, in the stray light of the lamp, her moss-green clothes remained dry.

Setting his quill aside, Halsedric dug out the earthen cup that held the beer he reserved for the huntress. Taking both mug and loaf, he lifted them in anticipation of Herodiani's approach.

After removing her quiver of arrows and her sword, Herodiani strode over and accepted her meal. She sat cross-legged next to Halsedric and sniffed the contents of the mug.

"Ale?" she said in her high, sweet voice

"As good as any," Halsedric answered as he picked up the quill from the ground. He then returned to the half-decoded message that rested in his lap.

She took a sip and set the mug down on the ground next to her. Pulling back the edges of the cloth that covered her bread, she tore a large hunk from the brown loaf before covering it again.

"Anything of note?" asked Halsedric, distracted, his eyes fixed on the document before him.

She swallowed a mouthful of the ale before answering, "Nothing moves this night. Not in this weather."

At once, Halsedric turned his attention to Roe. "So, by what course will you take us to the Wychwood? North to the river?"

"Aye," answered Roe with a nod. Having secured a victory over one buzzing pest, he thought it best to rest for the next trial. He leaned back and clasped his fingers across his chest. Beneath the blanket, the hay sighed and squeaked. "I have a camp near there. At the north of the wood, and west."

Halsedric was amazed. "I thought you said—"

"Most of the Wychwood is as they say," interrupted Roe, his head turning slightly toward Halsedric. "But the lands where I trap ain't so. The wood there is thick with willow, aspen, and birch. It's lowlands and fens, mostly reeds and streams closer to the wash of the Orem. A prime spot for water game. That's where I get pelts for the furriers in the city. The camp ain't much. Naught but a shelter for my beasts and me. I ain't had no troubles there. Further in is where the name for the Wychwood come. The farmers tell no lie. 'Tis a place only fools venture.

Later this season I was going to head up there to harvest a few pelts. Them's the ones I take into the city. Been other trappers up there in the past—I've found camps. I reckon they're old. Mayhaps, they left when the beaver ran low. Mayhaps not."

"You would say a northern approach is safe?" said Herodiani as she chewed her crust of bread.

"For the most? Aye. Ain't had no troubles takin' that route." Right after answering, Roe's head turned and his face changed, his brows knitting for a moment. He went to speak, then halted.

"There is more?" asked Halsedric.

Roe hesitated to answer. "Well, it's...my second season up in them parts, and some raven came 'round to the camp."

"A raven, you say?" Halsedric's interest was piqued, his pale eyes now fixed on Roe.

"Them birds are common in these parts, 'specially so, when there's game bein' dressed and hides bein' tanned. Carrion fowl come lookin' for a quick meal. Yet, this thing was...unnatural, if'n you know what I mean."

"How so?" interjected Herodiani.

Roe's head tilted to one side as he summoned the words to say. "The bird was big, for one. As big as an eagle. It mostly comes on the day next, when I've settled in. The horses don't like it. And that thing drives away all the other fowl—not even a sparrow song can be heard. When it shows, that place gets mighty quiet."

Halsedric's eyes met those of Herodiani in an intense and wordless conversation. The events at the Horn of Torgiv were still fresh in their memories.

"And it don't do nothin'," Roe continued, heedless of the reaction of the others. "Just sits on a perch, watchin'. Even when I'm cleanin' the pelts and castin' the fat into the weeds—it don't come down. It just stares, them eyes followin' me from trap to trap."

After a time, Roe looked up and noticed the reaction of Halsedric and the Elanni huntress. "What?" he asked, confused.

Halsedric broke from Herodiani's stare. His words were not hastily offered, as if he had to push his way through the many thoughts buzzing about in his mind. "We saw such a creature on our excursion to the Horn of Torgiv."

"You saw such a beast?"

"Yes," answered Halsedric with a shallow nod.

"I slew one," added Herodiani, after which the conversation fell silent.

Eyes growing wide, Roe looked at the pair, bewildered by the silence. "And?"

"It was no raven, but a dark sorcerer. Or something akin to such things," replied Halsedric.

Herodiani was the first to break the sudden lull in the discourse. "If it is there, we cannot enter the forest by means of the northern camp. I would avoid, also, the course of the Orem."

"Even to follow the Upper Orem?" said the trapper.

Roe's question was quickly answered by Halsedric. "If your camp has been discovered, then it is safe to assume that the means of your approach may be known. I agree with Herodiani on this. A different path must be taken." He then looked at Roe with an inquisitive stare. "You have sought other approaches to the Wychwood, yes?"

"Aye," answered Roe. "Several streams cut the wood. There's another that splits the southern end. If'n we can't approach from my camp, then we swing wide across the eastern wilds 'till we hit the waters. Then follow that back 'till the fringe of the wood. Make camp on the fair side of the woods. Head east on the day next."

"How long of a ride—" asked Herodiani, before Roe cut in.

"Ain't no ridin'. It's hard enough to keep my beasts tame in the camp, and they don't want no part of them woods. If'n we go, it'll be on foot. I'll have to leave my beasts here, as should you."

Herodiani spoke to Halsedric in the flowing sing-song tongue of her people. Halsedric acknowledged her words with a nod, then turned his attention to Roe. "How long of a march?"

"About the same. A day to make the shallow creek, two days to make the shore of the West Bramble. Then we follow the river's course north. Mayhaps two, dependin' on the weather and how fast we move."

Halsedric gazed once more outside the barn. The sound of the water falling was mesmerizing, lulling him into deep thought.

"Very well," answered Halsedric. "In the morning, we depart on foot."

Stay tuned for

The Revenant and the Cult Book Two:

The Terror in the Wychwood

Thank you for reading *The Revenant and the Cult, Book 1: The Trapper and the Missing Spy*. I hope you enjoyed it.

Now that you've completed the story, please consider leaving a review. Reviews are considered essential feedback for authors and are used by readers to make purchasing decisions.

If you liked this book, perhaps consider these other releases by Herman P. Hunter:

The Revenant and the Tomb (2022)
The Wizard's Stone (2023)

Heavily influenced by pulp fiction, epic fantasy, the Bible, Dungeons and Dragons, and even the occasional scary movie, Herman P. Hunter seeks to blend these influences into every story he writes.

Milton Keynes UK
Ingram Content Group UK Ltd.
UKHW021134130524
442628UK00014B/622